The cruelty of strangers . . .

Hesitantly Marissa walked to the front of the room. She had been in the very back, surrounded by me, Cindy, and Veronica. Now Krystal and the other cheerleaders really saw Marissa's face for the first time.

"Oh, no," Krystal gasped, before she could stop herself.

"My name is Marissa," Marissa said through the hole that passed for a mouth. I could feel how deeply embarrassed she was.

"Can you, like, move around okay?" Krystal asked her. The look on her face was one of complete horror.

"I can move around fine," Marissa said in her funny, nasal voice. "I mean, I know I don't look like a cheerleader..."

Krystal cut her off. "There's only one thing you need to know," she told Marissa. "Cheerleading is tough. You have to have the spirit. You have to work hard."

"I can work hard," Marissa assured her.

"Well, then, if you've got the spirit and you work hard, you can be a cheerleader. Now, this is how the cheer goes," Krystal said. She put her hands on her hips, one pom-pom in each hand, and she began to cheer.

The Accident

For Tisha Hamilton, my editor,
and Regula Noetzli, my agent—
the unsung heroines behind my books.
Thanks.

Published by Troll Communications L.L.C.

Printed in the United States of America.
10 9 8 7 6 5 4 3 2 1

HOPE HOSPITAL

The Accident

BY CHERIE BENNETT

Troll

Chapter 1

"Let's talk about guys," I suggested to my two best friends, Cindy Winters and Veronica Langley.

It was Saturday morning, and we were hanging out in my bedroom before we went over to Hope Hospital, where we all do volunteer work. Cindy and Veronica had slept over the night before. It had been a blast, and my wrecked room told the tale.

"That's all you ever want to talk about," Cindy said, reaching for a handful of M&M's from the extra large package we hadn't quite polished off the night before.

"It's nine o'clock in the morning,"

Veronica said, making a face at Cindy. "How can you eat candy?"

Cindy shrugged and dumped a few more M&M's into her mouth. "My stomach doesn't care what time it gets a chocolate fix."

"Don't you think Brad and I make a darling couple?" I asked my friends eagerly, rolling over onto my back to stare up at the ceiling. The ceiling of my bedroom looks like cottage cheese, so I closed my eyes and pictured Brad's face, instead.

I had met Brad a couple of weeks earlier, when we had both been patients at Hope Hospital in the tiny town of Hope, Michigan. That's where we live. My family moved here from San Francisco when I was nine. That's when my dad got his doctorate in child psychology, and he got a job at Hope.

I have lupus—this autoimmune disease where my body's immune system turns on itself. It's kind of hard to explain. Sometimes I'm so tired I can hardly get out of bed. Sometimes I run fevers, and my joints hurt. Sometimes scary stuff happens to my blood, or to my internal organs. I've spent a lot of time in the hospital because of all this.

Don't worry. It's not contagious.

Having lupus and being sick some of the time does not exactly help out my social life. But the true nail in the old coffin is the fact that I am home-schooled. *Home-schooled!* With my two bratty little sisters and my bratty little brother. My mother teaches us in our garage, which my parents converted into a school.

Why, you might ask, am I forced to endure this? Well, you see, my family is Chinese. My grandparents, who live with us, are from Singapore. They are very old-fashioned and strict. According to my grandparents, I should not even talk to a boy until I'm, like, twenty-five, and then only if we're already engaged. And, of course, this guy has to be Chinese.

There are not a lot of Chinese guys in Hope, Michigan.

The other thing is that everyone in my family thinks the most important thing in life is education. And my parents don't think Hope has very good schools. They came to this conclusion when I was in the fifth grade, and I spent most of the year out in the hallway tutoring kids who were falling behind. My parents had a total fit when they found out.

So, since my mom has a teaching degree, they came up with the brilliant solution of having mom teach us at home. My whole family pitched in and converted the garage into this family school. And I've been going there for two years now.

So I ask you, how was I ever supposed to meet any guys? How was I ever supposed to meet *anyone*? My life was one big bore.

Until a few weeks ago, when everything changed.

I was a patient at Hope, on the Foxx Wing—which is where all the teenage patients are—because I was having some problems with my blood, because of my lupus.

I know this will sound bizarre, but actually being in the hospital isn't always so awful. I mean, at least there are different people to meet. It sure beats going to school in my *garage*! I know the staff really well, and everyone is nice to me. I know all the dish, too, such as which nurses are secretly in love with which doctors. And I always hang out with the little kids in pediatrics. I just like kids, I guess.

But, anyway, this time when I got admitted, I met Brad. Brad Kennedy. He's medium height and thin, with straight blondish hair that falls in his eyes. He was painting in the teen lounge—it's called the Foxes Den after Jeremy Foxx, this TV star who donated all the money for the wing—and I walked right over to him and introduced myself.

You might think that having no social life I would be shy, but just the opposite is true. I figure no guts, no glory, you know what I mean?

Well, Brad was really nice but kind of shy. He said he was fourteen—one year older than me—and that he went to a private boys' school nearby. We talked about music—he's a big alternative music fan—and we got along really well.

I asked him why he was in the hospital—like I said, I'm not shy—but he didn't tell me. Well, aside from being kind of thin and pale he didn't look that sick or anything, so I just let the whole thing drop.

Anyway, the day after that I met Cindy Winters (her real name is *Cinderella*—can you believe it?) and Veronica Langley, these two thirteen-year-old girls who were both at the hospital to visit Cindy's little sister, Heidi, who had fallen out of a Ferris wheel at a fair. How horrible is *that*?

And I guess you could say that meeting Cindy and Veronica changed my life.

"I cannot understand why you spend your time daydreaming about boys," Veronica said, breaking into my thoughts.

"Not boys, a certain boy," I qualified, rolling over onto my stomach. "Brad is so...so..."

"Gag me," Cindy put in, reaching for some bubble gum on the dresser. She tore it open to read the comic the gum was wrapped in, then popped it into her mouth.

"You wouldn't say 'gag me' if we were talking about Trevor," I pointed out.

Cindy didn't say anything, because she knew I was right. Trevor Wayne is this guy friend of hers, who she really, really, really wants to be more than just a friend, if you catch my drift.

"Maybe Brad will be my first real boyfriend," I daydreamed.

"Tina, do you think Brad is lying around right now daydreaming about you?" Veronica asked me, sitting up and crossing her legs.

"I sure hope so," I replied seriously.

"Probably not," Veronica qualified, "even if he does like you. Because boys do not make girls the center of their lives."

"So, neither do girls," Cindy said, blowing a huge bubble and popping it. She opened the pizza box and looked inside. Nothing but crust. "I wish we had some pizza left."

"Cold pizza?" Veronica asked, aghast.

"Sure," Cindy said, "it makes a great breakfast."

"Medical science should study your stomach," Veronica said seriously.

You see, Cindy and Veronica could hardly be any more different from each other. It's kind of amazing that they got to be friends, actually.

Veronica had just moved to Hope from New York, because her parents had gotten a divorce and her mom had been made the new head of Pediatric Surgery at Hope Hospital. Cindy had lived in Hope her whole life. Her mom died from cancer, and her dad is a pediatric social worker at the hospital.

They had been assigned to do a project together for history class. Cindy is this cute, tiny blonde, a great gymnast, really funny and regular, and Veronica is this tall, gorgeous ballet dancer with perfect long brown hair, who seems kind of serious most of the time.

Oh, one other thing. Veronica is rich. I mean really, really rich. And Cindy is kind of poor. I guess my family is somewhere in between.

Oh, and one more thing. Trevor—the guy I told you about before, who is Cindy's friend—well, he seemed to be after Veronica. This didn't exactly add to Cindy's love for Veronica, if you follow me.

But after Heidi's horrible accident, Veronica had convinced her mom to do the surgery on Heidi, and I guess that was the beginning of Cindy not thinking that Veronica was so awful after all.

About Heidi's accident. It was such a terrible thing. Cindy was up in the Ferris wheel with her—in fact it was Cindy who had convinced Heidi to go on the ride. They had been up at the top of the wheel when Heidi dropped the cotton candy she was eating. She stood up to reach for it, and the safety bar that's supposed to hold you in the seat gave way, and Heidi fell from the top of the Ferris wheel to the ground.

At first no one was sure if Heidi would live. Veronica's mom had to do this really delicate surgery on her, and she had two broken legs and just all kinds of terrible injuries. But Heidi made it through the surgery, and it looked like even though she'd be in the hospital for a long time, she was going to be okay.

Cindy, Veronica, and I spent a lot of time at the hospital visiting Heidi. (Of course, since I was a patient myself, I didn't have very far to go!) We hung out with the little kids in pediatrics—they are so cute.

Everything seemed like it was fine. Heidi was getting better. Brad liked me. He even said we should hang out when we both got out of the hospital. So what could be bad?

Then something really horrible happened. One of the little kids we'd gotten to be friends with in the pediatric unit died. She had leukemia, and we knew she was really sick. But we had just talked to her that afternoon. Brianna had been in Heidi's room, and they got to be friends. One minute she was this cute little kid who told us she wasn't going to die, and the next minute she was...dead.

She was only five years old.

Brianna's funeral was maybe the worst experience of my life. It was even worse for Cindy. She had had to live through her mom's death from cancer, and then her little sister's accident. When Brianna died,

Cindy just lost it. It was like she just couldn't take one more awful thing happening. I didn't know what I could possibly say to her to make her feel any better. I mean, all the words seemed so empty and stupid.

Veronica felt the same way, so we just stayed with Cindy and didn't say very much at all.

Before Brianna died, we had been planning to put on this variety show for the sick little kids at the hospital. Cindy did the bravest thing I think I've ever seen anyone do. Even though she was grieving for her mom and for Brianna, too, she went ahead and did the show because she knew both of them would want her to.

And then—this is really amazing—she came up with this idea. She said we should keep coming to the hospital, to do stuff for the kids there. I guess it was Cindy's way of trying to have something good come out of her mom's and Brianna's deaths.

Something about everything that happened made the three of us feel really close to each other. It's hard to explain. I mean, we're as different from one another as we could possibly be, but we became not just friends but best friends. More like sisters.

Now we go to the hospital almost every day. The little kids there love us, and we love them right back.

By the way, Brad was still a patient, and I still didn't know what was wrong with him! Since he was Veronica's cousin, I was working on her to tell me.

"So, what's wrong with Brad?" I asked Veronica, pulling myself out of my reverie. I reached for the last of the M&M's.

"As I have told you a hundred times," Veronica said in her proper voice, "you have to ask him yourself."

"I did, he just didn't tell me," I reminded her. "How can you be my friend if you won't even tell me a secret?"

"It's not a secret," Veronica maintained. "I just think that he has the right to tell you himself." Her stomach growled loud enough for me to hear. "Want to go downstairs and get some breakfast?"

I threw a half-full bag of barbecue potato chips at her. "Here, eat."

"You know I don't eat junk food," Veronica said.

"You're not human," Cindy said, flipping through the pages of a teen magazine. She blew another huge bubble and popped it with her tongue. "Look at this article. 'How to Plan the Perfect Wedding.' I'd like to have my first date before I plan my wedding, thank you very much."

"I know just what my wedding gown is going to look like," I told her, putting my hands behind my head. "It'll be white—"

"Good start!" Cindy quipped.

"—imported Belgian lace," I continued, "with one of those trains that six little girls have to carry for me—"

"I'm not getting married until I'm really old," Cindy said firmly.

"I'm not getting married at all," Veronica put in.

I rolled over on my stomach. "Really?"

"How can you know that when you're thirteen?" Cindy pointed out.

"Because I know what I want and what I don't want," Veronica said with a shrug. "I don't want to be tied down. And I don't want some man telling me what I can or can't do."

"Marriage doesn't have to be like that," I said. "My father doesn't tell my mother what to do."

"Your mother stays home and teaches in a garage," Veronica reminded me. "Your father is the one who gets to go out and have a career."

"Good point," I muttered.

"Besides, nobody ever stays in love with anybody," Veronica continued.

"I don't think that's true," I said, sitting up on my bed. "I mean, my parents still love each other."

"How do you know?" Veronica asked.

I thought about that for a moment. In my culture, parents don't openly show affection to each other. I had never seen my parents really kiss passionately or anything.

Well, who would want to see that? Yuck.

"Look at my parents," Veronica continued. "I thought they really loved each other. And then one day—*bam*—it's over. They hate each other. Now they're getting a divorce and they say terrible things about each other all the time."

"My parents loved each other," Cindy said in a low voice.

I looked at her. She was examining a hangnail. How horrible, was all I could think, to have your mom die when you're just a little kid. A lot of the time I can't stand my mother, but if anything ever happened to her, I would want to die, too.

"You guys, let's go back to the subject of Brad," I suggested, since I wanted to lighten things up. “Do you think he really likes me?”

“He likes you,” Veronica said.

“How do you know?” I demanded.

“He told me so.”

I jumped off my bed and landed on the edge of her sleeping bag, where I grabbed both her hands and screamed, “He told you so? He actually for real told you so?”

“Yes,” Veronica confirmed. “Yesterday.”

“Oh my God, he really likes me!” I screamed. “Maybe he thinks about me as much as I think about him! Tell me everything he said to you, word for word.”

But before Veronica could tell me, the door to my bedroom opened. There stood my grandmother, and all four feet eleven inches was clearly furious.

“What all this noise?” she demanded, folding her arms.

“Sorry, Grandma,” I said meekly, always the obedient child.

Then she saw the disastrous state of my room. I looked around as she did. There were tapes strewn everywhere. Junk food spilled out onto the white carpet. A bunch of clothes we had tried on lay in a heap on the floor. The empty pizza box had turned over, so that a blotch of tomato sauce now stained the rug.

Oops.

"You girls get up now," Grandma said. "Clean up disaster. Tina Wu, you are pig!"

"Sorry, Grandma," I said again. No one can make me feel as small as my tiny grandmother.

"Tina Wu, this unacceptable!" she insisted. Her eyes blazed into mine, and she turned on her heel and left.

My grandmother has this thing where she always calls me by my first and last names. I have no idea why.

"We'll help you clean up," Veronica offered, gracefully getting up from her sleeping bag.

"Sure, Tina Wu," Cindy teased.

"Thanks," I said.

Quickly we all got up and began to clean up my room. But as bad as I felt about getting yelled at by Grandma, nothing could change the joy in my heart.

Brad Kennedy liked me.

Just then the phone rang near my bed. It's not my own phone—my parents refuse to let me have one; it's an extension.

I picked it up quickly. "Wu residence," I said.

My parents force me to answer the phone this way.

"Hi, Tina, it's Dr. Dan," a friendly male voice said.

Dr. Dan is Cindy's dad. He's not really a doctor—this is just the pet name the kids at the hospital have given him.

"Hi, Dr. Dan," I said. "Want to speak to Cindy?"

"No, actually," he said. "You girls are coming over here this afternoon, aren't you?"

"Yeah, in about an hour, I think," I told him.

"Good," Dr. Dan said. "Could you stop into room 347? There's a little girl in there who just got admitted yesterday. Her name is Marissa Ruiz. She's eight."

I grabbed a piece of paper from my nightstand and wrote down the information.

"I got it," I told Dr. Dan. "We'll be there."

"She's having kind of a hard time with the other kids," Dr. Dan continued.

"But they're usually so nice to each other," I said.

"I know," Dr. Dan agreed. "But Marissa is...well, she's different."

"Different how?" I asked.

"She was in a fire," Dr. Dan explained. "She was pretty badly burned..."

"So she's funny looking?" I wondered

aloud. "Usually the little kids are pretty okay with stuff like that."

"Usually," Dr. Dan said. "But not this time."

"How come?"

"Because...there's no delicate way to put this," Dr. Dan said. "Marissa Ruiz looks like a monster."

"He actually said she looks like a monster?" Veronica asked me, as we hurried down the corridor of Hope Hospital on our way to visit Marissa Ruiz.

"That's what he said," I confirmed. "She was in some kind of a fire, I guess."

"I can't believe my dad would ever say something like that," Cindy said, stopping to retie the laces on her high-tops.

"I know, it was weird," I agreed. "Your father is so, so..."

"Nice," Veronica put in. "Silly, but nice."

That was true. Cindy's dad acted like a big kid himself a lot of the time.

"I'm sure he was exaggerating," I decided as we turned the corner to the pediatric wing. We came to room 347, and I knocked.

"Come in," a little voice said. The voice sounded kind of muffled, like someone with a really awful cold.

The three of us walked into the room and then stopped dead. I tried so hard not to stare.

Because Dr. Dan had been right, the little girl in the bed looked like a monster.

Oh, she had on really nice clothes—a bright pink corduroy jumper with a white turtleneck underneath. And she had beautiful glossy black curls tied back with a white ribbon. And she had the prettiest black eyes.

But the rest of her face. Oh, her face was so terrible. Where there should have been a nose, there was just a small piece of flesh with an opening at the bottom. Then scar tissue attached that lump of flesh to what would have been her lips, if she had had any.

But she didn't.

There was just a hole there, for her mouth.

"Hello," she said, in her nasal, muffled voice. "I'm Marissa." She put down the pad of paper she'd been drawing on.

I gulped hard. "I'm Tina, and this is Cindy and Veronica," I said, trying to sound as normal as possible.

Because she didn't have any lips, she couldn't really smile, and yet I could see the smile in her eyes. She looked at Cindy. "Oh, you're Dr. Dan's daughter, right? He told me his daughter would be the blond one!"

"That's me," Cindy said with forced cheerfulness.

"Thanks for coming to visit me," Marissa said. "I was lonely."

None of us could think of anything to say to that. *Of course* the kid was lonely. Anyone who saw her would probably scream. *I* wanted to scream. I didn't like myself for it, but I'm telling you the truth.

"I'm having surgery," Marissa continued. "In four days. I'm getting a new nose!"

"That's wonderful," Veronica managed.

"That's what I was drawing," Marissa said. "How I'm going to look. Want to see?"

The three of us gathered around the pad of paper she'd been drawing on. She had drawn a pretty little girl with black curls and shining eyes. And a perfect nose and mouth. "That's what I used to look like," she explained.

I got a big lump in my throat and I swallowed hard. "That's great," I told her. "You can really draw!"

"Thanks," Marissa said. "Hey, I bet I could draw you!"

"You think so?" I asked her.

"Well, maybe not perfectly, but I could try."

"Okay, I'll be your model," I said. I sat in the chair near her bed. "You want profile or front view?"

"Well, how are you today?" Rachel Dander chirped from the doorway.

Rachel is a pediatric nurse. She's cute, in a bouncy kind of way, with long blond hair and big eyes. But she's so sticky-icky sweet that she brings out the worst in me. Cindy, too.

Of course, that might be because Rachel is secretly dating Cindy's father. Cindy doesn't want to believe it's true, but it is. I told you, I know all the hospital gossip.

"You have visitors, how super!" Rachel exclaimed. She looked at Cindy. "Hi, Cindy, sweetie. How's your daddy?"

"You ought to know, you see him here every day," Cindy said in a nasty voice.

"Well, that's true, I do!" Rachel agreed happily.

Nothing seems to offend her. Sometimes

I wonder if maybe she's not the brightest thing on earth.

"Say, I've got a wonderful idea," Rachel said. "Why don't you all come down to the lounge? There's going to be a ventriloquist!"

"No, thank you," Marissa said in a little voice.

"But you'll love it!" Rachel insisted. "Ventriloquists are so funny! See, he makes his dummy talk—"

Marissa shook her head no. "No one likes me there."

Rachel came over to Marissa's bed and sat down. "Sure they do."

"Kids never like me," Marissa said, "ever since...well, you know." There was no self-pity in her voice. "I scare them."

"Well, you should do what you want to do, that's what I think," Cindy said. "If the kids get to know you, they won't be scared anymore."

"I never saw a ventriloquist..." Marissa said wistfully, "but—"

"We'll all be with you," Veronica told her.

"Right," I agreed. "You won't be alone."

"Terrific!" Rachel cried, clapping her hands together. "Well, I'll see the four of you down there, then! This is super!" She bounced out of the room.

"You can draw me when we get back to your room," I suggested, as Marissa got up from her bed.

"Maybe I shouldn't go down there," she said, hanging back. "I went there yesterday and...a bunch of kids ran out of the lounge. One little boy cried."

"We'll be with you this time," Cindy said firmly. "The other kids need a chance to get to know you."

"That always happens when you're different," I told her.

"I know," she agreed. "Different is what I've always been."

"Hi, boys and girls, I'm the Amazing Arnold!" the ventriloquist cried. He looked like he was in his fifties or sixties—old. He was a short guy with a big round stomach, and he had on the ugliest green tie I ever saw in my life. "And this..." he pulled a dummy out of a big black box, "is my friend, Garbonzo Bill! Say hello, Garbonzo!"

The dummy had on the same ugly green tie that Amazing Arnold was wearing. Garbonzo Bill looked around at the audience of about twenty kids, six staffers, and us.

"Hi, kids!" Garbonzo Bill yelled.

The whole thing about a ventriloquist is that when he makes his dummy talk, he doesn't move his own mouth, so it seems like the dummy is really talking.

Only the Amazing Arnold moved his lips. A lot.

"So, Garbonzo Bill," Arnold said, "aren't these a fine-looking bunch of boys and girls?"

"Yeah!" Garbonzo said, and it was perfectly clear that it was really Arnold who was saying it.

"So, Garbonzo, tell us what you did today for fun," Arnold asked his dummy.

"Came here with you!" Garbonzo replied. "You know that, you brought me here!" Arnold looked at the audience. "That was a joke!" he told them. "Right, Garbonzo?"

"How would I know, I'm a dummy!" the dummy said.

"Hey, man, I can see your lips moving!" Jerome yelled.

I stifled a laugh. Trust Jerome to tell the truth.

Jerome is ten years old. He's this really smart, cute little African-American kid who pretends he's street tough, even though he's rich and gets straight A's at a private school. He also has bone cancer, and he only has one leg. In fact, the cancer has spread, and for a while it looked as if they were going to have to remove his other foot as well. But for now they have put off removing his other foot, and he is on an experimental new drug, instead.

"Me too!" Deena yelled out, then she giggled and covered her mouth with her hand. Deena is four. She has brittle diabetes and the doctors can't seem to stabilize her. She has become good friends with Cindy's little sister, Heidi, who sat next to her in her wheelchair, her broken legs suspended from portable pulleys. Deena and Heidi are both madly in love with Jerome.

"Hey, Garbonzo, who invited the kids to be in the act?" Arnold asked his dummy.

"Not me!" the dummy replied as Arnold moved his lips.

As the Amazing Arnold continued his truly awful act, I looked around at the little kids. Some of the really young ones were into it, but the older kids were restless. Which meant that they turned to stare at Marissa. A ten-year-old girl named Kimber, who was having foot surgery, stared at Marissa and then whispered to her older sister. Even two of the nurse's aides were staring and whispering. Marissa kept her eyes glued on Arnold, but somehow I knew she was just pretending not to notice people staring at her.

"Well, wasn't that super?" Rachel cried when Arnold finished his act. She ran over to Arnold and clapped her hands with enthusiasm.

"But I'm not done!" Arnold exclaimed. "I have another dummy, and this whole great thing worked out where one of the dummies gets locked in the box, and—"

"Well, we'll sure look forward to having you come back another time to show us that!" Rachel said.

"Hey, I volunteer to take my time to come down here and entertain these sick kids—" Arnold was saying, clearly ticked off.

"And we sure do appreciate it!" Rachel said.

"I didn't charge you," the Amazing Arnold went on. "I did it for charity, you know!"

"Now, boys and girls, how about another round of applause for the Amazing Arnold!" Rachel cried.

"You stink, man," Jerome called out. "Go back to dummy school!"

"Now, Jerome—" Rachel chided, turning red from embarrassment. "The Amazing

Arnold is our friend—"

"He's lame," Jerome said, shaking his head. "Seriously lame."

"Yeah, lame!" Heidi agreed.

The Amazing Arnold packed up his stuff and left in a huff. Rachel turned on the television set. There was a football game on.

"No football!" Deena insisted. "I hate when my dad watches football!"

"The football stays!" Jerome said.

"Now, Jerome—" Rachel began.

"I say the football stays, woman!" Jerome repeated.

While Rachel and Jerome argued about football, more and more kids turned to stare at Marissa. One boy stared hard, and then he made a face and pretended to shudder. The boy sitting with him laughed. Kimber pointed at Marissa and whispered to her sister behind a cupped hand.

At first Marissa pretended she didn't notice the kids watching her. She acted like she was fascinated by the football game. But after a while she began to slink down in her chair, her eyes looking sadder and sadder by the second.

I knew we should do something, but I didn't know what. I traded looks with

Cindy and Veronica. They didn't seem to know what to do, either.

"Ooh, cheerleaders!" Heidi yelled, pointing to the TV screen.

I looked. There was a close-up of the Dallas Cowgirl Cheerleaders, doing a dance routine.

"I'm gonna be a cheerleader when I grow up," Heidi said, her eyes glued to the screen.

Now all the little girls in the room were looking at the TV again, instead of at Marissa.

"I'm trying out for cheerleading when I get to middle school," Kimber said, staring at the screen.

"I wish I could do cheerleading," Marissa said softly.

"You can," I assured her.

"No, I couldn't," Marissa replied. "Cheerleaders are always beautiful."

"That lets you out," the little boy who had been making faces at Marissa whispered to his friend.

Unfortunately, we could all hear him. I truly wanted to kill him.

"Really good cheerleaders are athletes and gymnasts," Veronica said. "It's not as easy as it looks."

"I can do a cartwheel," Kimber said eagerly. "After my surgery I'll be able to do it again!"

"Hey, did we tell you that Cindy is a gymnast?" I asked Marissa in a deliberately loud voice. Deena overheard me and toddled over to us.

"She's my sister, you know," Heidi called out to them. "She's the best at gymnastics in the whole world!"

"Like in the Olympics?" Marissa asked.

"Can you do the balance beam?" said Kimber. Her sister wheeled Kimber's wheelchair closer to us.

"Well, I'm not as good as they are—" Cindy began.

"She is, too!" Heidi insisted.

"Yeah," Marielle agreed, wheeling her wheelchair closer. "We saw her in a show." Marielle was a beautiful little African-American girl with sickle-cell anemia, a disease that made her painfully thin and very weak.

That was true. We had put on our variety show at the hospital just a couple of weeks earlier.

"She's terrific," Veronica told Marissa.

"Right!" I agreed. "Cindy could have been, like, head cheerleader at her school, if she wanted to be!"

Cindy shot me a look that said "You are so full of it," but I ignored her.

"Does she have a cheerleading outfit?" Deena asked eagerly.

"Yeah!" Marissa added.

"Because you have to have the outfit or you aren't really a cheerleader," Marielle explained seriously.

"Right," Kimber agreed.

"Well, no," I admitted. The little girls looked crestfallen. "But...she's friends with all the cheerleaders at her school!" I added.

Now Cindy looked at me like I had truly lost my mind.

"Could we meet them?" Marissa asked hopefully, staring at Cindy. Heidi, Marielle, Deena, Kimber, and Kimber's sister stared at her hopefully, too.

Which meant they weren't staring at Marissa. Which is exactly what I wanted.

"I don't think—" Cindy began.

"Sure!" I exclaimed, interrupting Cindy. "In fact, Cindy's going to get her friends the cheerleaders to come over and teach you guys how to be cheerleaders!"

All the little girls cheered.

"My sister can do anything!" Heidi yelled happily.

It was great. No one was staring at Marissa. And everyone looked happy and excited.

Except for Cindy, that is. She looked like she was ready to kill me.

"I can't believe you said that!" Cindy exploded, as she and Veronica and I headed for the Foxes Den. "What you told those kids was a total lie! I don't hang with the cheerleaders from Hope Middle School, you know!"

It was an hour later. We had taken a very excited Marissa back to her room, where she drew my picture and then Veronica's picture. She really had talent. We taped the pictures up over her bed. Now we were on our way to the teen lounge, where we were going to meet Brad and Trevor.

I mentioned Trevor Wayne before—

Cindy's friend. And Trevor likes Cindy, too. Only maybe he likes Veronica even more.

What do you do if the guy you like seems to like one of your best friends better than he likes you? (I don't have an answer—but if you do you can write to me, Tina Wu, and give me your best advice. Thank you.)

Trevor is extremely darling. He's got really cute straight brown hair that kind of falls in his eyes. He's your basic babe.

Anyway, he and Cindy have been buds for years. But he asked Veronica out. Veronica won't go out with him, because Cindy is her friend. The whole thing is kind of complicated. Boy, was I glad that Brad was Veronica's cousin. I sure wouldn't want to try and compete with someone that gorgeous!

"Can you imagine how tough Marissa's life must be, looking like that?" Veronica said. "She must be miserable all the time."

"But did you see the look on her face when I told her Cindy's friends would come to the hospital to do a cheerleading exhibition?" I pointed out.

"My friends, that's a good one," Cindy snorted.

"And the other little girls got so excited

about the cheerleaders that they forgot to stare at Marissa," Veronica added softly.

"It was like for just a moment she was one of them," I continued as we rounded the corner. "Just another little girl in the hospital—"

"But she isn't just another little girl in the hospital," Cindy said, "and we all know it."

"But if the other kids spend time with her—like at this cheerleading thing—they'll get used to her, and they won't make her feel like she's a freak anymore," I said.

"So *you* invite some cheerleaders to the hospital, then," Cindy groused.

"I don't know any," I said cheerfully. "My grandmother can do a cartwheel, believe it or not, but I don't think that's what they have in mind."

As we got closer to the Foxes Den, I started to feel a little nervous. Not that I'm usually nervous around guys, because I'm not. But Brad is really special.

I caught my reflection in the glass at the nurses' station, and wondered if I looked okay. I had on red denim overalls and a red and white T-shirt with peace symbols all over it. Red is my favorite color. I also had on mascara and some cherry-flavored lip gloss. I almost always wear mascara. I feel like my eyes are so deep-set that you can't even see them if I don't.

Cindy tells me this is ridiculous—she never wears makeup. She has a very natural kind of style. At that moment she had on jeans and an oversized blue and white flannel shirt.

I looked over at Veronica, who always manages to look perfect. She had on pale pink cashmere leggings and a matching pale pink sweater. Her hair was in a French braid. She is so naturally gorgeous that the whole concept of makeup is lost on her.

If she wasn't my friend, I would have to hate her.

"Wait, I need some perfume," I told my friends, and I stopped to rummage around in my purse for some.

"You do not," Cindy insisted.

I ignored her and sprayed myself all over. "Want some?"

"Not me," Cindy said. "I hate that stuff."

"No thanks," Veronica said. "I already have on some rose oil from The Body Store."

Cindy looked over at Veronica out of the corner of her eye. "I wonder if Trevor likes roses," she mumbled.

Veronica gave Cindy a serious look. "I'm not wearing it for him."

"Yeah, well, the air is free, and he gets to sniff you, anyway," Cindy pointed out.

"There they are," I said as we walked into the Foxes Den. Trevor and Brad were across the room, looking at some CDs. We had introduced them to each other the week before, and they were already friends. Trevor didn't seem to mind that Brad was a patient in the hospital. I wondered all over again what was wrong with Brad.

"Hi, you guys!" I exclaimed, running over to them.

"Hi," Brad said, giving me his shy smile. My heart totally melted.

"What are you guys up to?" Cindy asked casually, plopping down on an overstuffed chair. She swung one of her legs over the side.

"Did you see the CD collection they've got here?" Trevor asked, shaking some hair out of his face. "I would kill for a collection like this!"

"There's a fund," Veronica explained, sitting down on the couch. "They get new CDs every few months—that's what one of the nurses told me."

Trevor sat down next to her. I could tell that Cindy was pretending not to mind. Brad and I sat down, too.

"So, how are the little kids doing?" Trevor asked.

"There's a new girl who got admitted yesterday," Veronica told him. "She was in a bad fire, and she has terrible facial scars."

"Bummer," Trevor said.

Veronica nodded in agreement. "She's this really beautiful little girl. It's so sad."

"But we've got a great plan to cheer her up!" I put in.

"*You* might call it great, Tina Wu," Cindy said, "*I* call it a pain in the butt."

Cindy had started calling me Tina Wu, just like my grandmother. I couldn't decide if I liked it or hated it.

"Why, what's the plan?" Brad asked.

I quickly explained how all the little girls—especially Marissa—loved cheerleaders, and how Cindy was going to get the cheerleaders from Hope Middle School to come to the hospital and do a cheerleading exhibition.

"You mean Dawn McKnight and Krystal Franklin?" Trevor asked, a smirk on his face. "Good luck!"

"Oh, come on," I said, "they're not going to say no to a bunch of sick little girls stuck in a hospital!"

"They might," Trevor said with a shrug.

"Cindy can get them to do it," I urged.

"Yeah, right," Cindy snorted. "We'd have a better shot if Trevor asked them. They are, like, constantly flirting with him."

"Great idea!" Veronica exclaimed.

"Now, wait a minute—" Trevor began.

"Oh, come on," I said, "it's for little kids—"

"If they'll listen to you, you should ask them," Brad agreed.

"Come on," Cindy wheedled. "Don't make me do it!"

We all stared hopefully at Trevor, until finally he laughed and gave in. "Okay, okay." He looked over at Cindy. "You and I will do it together, how's that?"

"Cool, big guy," Cindy said casually.

Although she was acting like it was no big thing, I knew that inside Cindy was turning cartwheels of happiness. She and Trevor were going to go to the cheerleaders together. It was almost, sort of like...well, like they were a couple. Wasn't it?

Just as we were finishing dinner that night, the phone rang. I knew that Cindy and Trevor had asked Trevor's older brother, Chris, if he'd drive them by cheerleading practice at school so they could talk to Dawn, Krystal, and the rest of the cheerleaders. And I figured the phone call was Cindy, letting me know what had happened.

I jumped up from the table, but before I could make a getaway, my grandmother stopped me.

"Tina Wu, sit down and eat," she commanded me, calmly chewing on her fish.

"But I know that's for me and it's really important—"

"Listen to your grandmother," my mother said, heaping some more rice on my plate.

I sighed in frustration as I heard the answering machine pick up. My little sisters, Amy and Sherry, and my little brother, Sam, all laughed and made faces at me.

"None of that at dinner table," my grandmother barked.

My little sisters and brother bit their lips to stop laughing. When Grandmother speaks, everyone listens.

"What you do at hospital today, Tina Wu?" Grandmother asked me.

"There's a new little girl who was in a fire," I explained, attempting to swallow some green beans, which I hate. "We took her to the kids' lounge."

"Good," Grandmother said.

"It's great that you're helping the kids there," my father said, smiling at me. "When a person has a disability, it's terrific therapy for them to help other people."

Sometimes I just want to kill my father.

"I don't have a disability," I said through clenched teeth.

"Tina, denial isn't helpful," he said mildly.

"Lupus isn't a disability," I insisted. "I'm perfectly normal."

He gave me that benign smile that makes me want to scream. It's a smile that says I'm-a-child-psychologist-and-I-know-better.

"May I be excused?" I asked hopefully.

Both my parents looked over at my grandmother to see if she would object. No one looked at my grandfather. He never objects to anything. He hardly ever talks, he just sits around reading old newspapers in Chinese.

Grandmother didn't say a word.

"You're excused," my mother said. "Be sure and do your homework tonight," she added.

"I will," I promised. One problem with having your mother for your teacher is that you can never lie and say you don't have any homework.

I ran upstairs to my room and quickly dialed Cindy's number.

"Hello?" It was Cindy's sixteen-year-old brother, Clark. He's named after Clark Kent, from the Superman comics. He's so cute. Unfortunately he has a girlfriend and he treats me like I'm about six years old.

"Hi, Clark, it's Tina."

"Oh, hi, kid," he said. "Hold on." Then he yelled for Cindy.

"Hello?" she said.

"Tell me everything," I demanded.

"You can hang up now, Clark," Cindy said.

I heard a click.

"He always tries to listen in," she explained. "Clark, are you still there?"

"He hung up; I heard him," I said impatiently. "Now, tell me what happened with the cheerleaders."

"Well, Chris drove us over to cheerleading practice—"

"I already *know* that part!"

"Right," she agreed. "Listen, do you think Trevor likes me?"

"You mean *likes* you–likes you?"

"Yeah."

"Well, I don't know," I said truthfully. "How did he treat you this afternoon?"

"Like he always treats me," Cindy said with a sigh.

"Maybe you need to get some sexy outfits or something," I suggested.

"Get real, Tina Wu," Cindy said. "First of all, I would never buy sexy clothes, because I think sexy clothes are not sexy. And second of all, I would look like a moron because I could practically buy my clothes in the kids' department."

"Still, we could work on your image..." I mused. "I mean, maybe it would, like, wake him up!"

"He's crazed for Veronica, I just know it," Cindy said with a sigh.

What could I say? I figured this was probably true.

"Well, anyway," I said, "what happened with the cheerleaders?"

"Trevor was great," Cindy reported. "Dawn was, like, all over him, and he didn't flirt back at all."

"Yeah, but what did they say?" I asked. "Will they come to the hospital or not?"

"She was so disgusting," Cindy continued. "I mean, she's supposed to be so in love with John Trinly, this really dumb jock at our school, so what's she doing flirting with Trevor?"

"But what did they say?" I asked. "Try to focus here."

"Don't you think it's totally obnoxious when a girl who has a boyfriend flirts with other guys?" Cindy demanded.

"Cindy! What did the cheerleaders say?" I yelled into the phone.

"Oh, they said yes," she said offhandedly.

"That's fantastic!" I cried. "How many of them are coming to the hospital and when?"

"Tomorrow afternoon," Cindy said. "And all eight of them are coming. Believe me, what Krystal tells them to do, they do. They're all such sheep!"

"You did great! I am so psyched!" I bounced up and down on my bed. "Marissa will love this, don't you think?"

"Yeah," Cindy agreed. "We have Trevor to thank for it. Krystal never would have said yes to me."

"I'll give him a big hug tomorrow," I promised.

Cindy sighed. "I wish I had the nerve to give him a big hug."

I laughed. "I'll give him one for you, how's that?"

Cindy laughed too. "Tina Wu, that is one message I'd like to deliver myself!"

Chapter 4

"WE ARE THE GIRLS FROM HOPE,
SO TAKE A NOTE!
WE WANT OUR GUYS TO SCORE,
POINTS GALORE!
WE'VE GOT THE TALENT AND DRIVE,
LOOK ALIVE!
REMEMBER OUR NAME,
WE'RE GONNA WIN THIS GAME!
H-O-P-E, HOPE, HOPE, HOPE!
YEAAAAHHHHHH!"

The Hope Middle School Cheerleaders finished another cheer, and all the girls in the hospital lounge clapped and cheered.

It was the next afternoon, and just as Cindy had predicted, all eight cheerleaders had showed up at the hospital. They all wore their blue and yellow cheerleading outfits and carried their blue and yellow pom-poms.

I barely had a chance to get introduced to Krystal before they started their cheerleading exhibition, but she seemed nice enough.

Ha. Was I wrong.

"Can you do a pyramid?" Marissa asked eagerly.

"Yeah!" Heidi squeaked with excitement. "Can you?"

"Sure," Krystal said, whipping her long auburn hair over her shoulder. She turned to the other girls on the team. "Okay, let's do the pyramid cheer."

"WE'RE GONNA TELL YA WHICH TEAM
IS IN
HOPE'S THE NAME, AND WE'RE
GONNA WIN!
WE'RE GONNA BUILD A PYRAMID
SO YOU CAN SEE
HOPE'S THE NAME THAT SPELLS
VIC-TOR-Y!"

As they cheered, three girls took their places and two other girls got on their shoulders. Then the littlest cheerleader got up on the top. Then Krystal and Dawn, the other head cheerleader, did cartwheels and splits in front of the pyramid. I have to admit, it was pretty impressive. Because of having lupus, sometimes my joints hurt and get weak. Sometimes I have trouble walking, much less building a pyramid or turning a cartwheel.

"That is so awesome," Kimber breathed.

"Can you show us how to do a cheer?" Deena asked eagerly.

"Yeah," Krystal said. "You guys come on up here with us."

Marielle's face fell and she bit her lower lip. "I can't get out of my wheelchair," she said.

"Me, neither," Heidi said.

"That's okay," Veronica said quickly, going over to Heidi. "Krystal will show you a cheer that can be done standing or sitting, right Krystal?"

"Yeah, I guess," Krystal said carelessly.

"Marissa can do the cheer standing, and Heidi and Marielle can do it sitting," I suggested. "And then the rest of you guys can learn to do it either way. How's that?"

"When I'm better I can do it standing," Marielle explained solemnly.

"Right," I agreed, though I could feel something twisting in my heart. Marielle was very, very sick. She might never *get* better.

"Go on up there," Cindy urged Marissa.

"I don't think I should," Marissa whispered.

"It's okay, Marissa," Cindy said gently. "You'll be great."

Hesitantly Marissa walked to the front of the room. She had been in the very back, surrounded by me, Cindy, and Veronica. Now Krystal and the other cheerleaders really saw Marissa's face for the first time.

"Oh my God," Krystal said, before she could stop herself.

I felt like such an idiot, letting Marissa go up there by herself like that. I looked over at Cindy and Veronica, and I could tell they felt badly, too. We should have prepared Krystal and the other cheerleaders. We should have handled it better.

But we didn't. And now it was too late.

"My name is Marissa," Marissa said through the hole that passed for a mouth. I could feel how deeply embarrassed she was.

"Can you, like, move around okay?"

Krystal asked her. The look on her face was one of horror.

"I can move around fine," Marissa said in her funny, nasal voice. "It's only my face that got burnt up." She turned to all the girls in the room who were staring at her. "And in a few days I'm going to have a new face."

"It's not your fault if you were in a fire," Heidi piped up. "Just like it's not my fault I had to get my head shaved on account of my accident, right?"

I could have kissed her.

Marissa looked gratefully at the little girl. "Right," she said. She looked at Krystal. "If it's okay with you, that is. I mean, I know I don't look like a cheerleader..."

Krystal stuck out her jaw and cut Marissa off. "There's only one thing you need to know," she told Marissa. "Cheerleading is tough. You have to have the spirit. You have to work hard."

"I can work hard," Marissa assured her.

"Well, then, if you've got the spirit and you work hard, you can be a cheerleader."

Marissa nodded solemnly. Was it my imagination or had Krystal been almost human for a moment there?

"Now, this is how the cheer goes," Krystal said. She put her hands on her hips, one pom-pom in each hand, and she began to cheer.

"WE'RE FROM HOPE AND WE
COULDN'T BE PROUDER
AND IF YA CAN'T HEAR US,
WE'LL CHEER A LITTLE LOUDER!
WE'RE FROM HOPE AND WE
COULDN'T BE PROUDER
AND IF YA CAN'T HEAR US,
WE'LL CHEER A LITTLE LOUDER!"

Then she did the cheerleader jump, where her legs went sideways, bent at the knees, and she jumped around and cheered.

"Okay, you girls try it," Dawn suggested, taking her place next to Krystal. The other cheerleaders lined up, too.

"Where should I stand?" Marissa asked shyly.

"Right here," the littlest cheerleader, Patti, said. Then she handed Marissa her pom-poms. I decided Patti was the cheerleader I liked the best.

Marissa stood next to Patti, and this time she joined in. Heidi and Marielle yelled from their wheelchairs. Every girl in the room, sitting or standing, joined in.

> "WE'RE FROM HOPE AND WE
> COULDN'T BE PROUDER
> AND IF YA CAN'T HEAR US,
> WE'LL CHEER A LITTLE LOUDER!"

Most of them couldn't jump—actually Marissa was about the only one who could—but they yelled and cheered as loudly as they could.

"You girls are fine!" I heard from the back of the room. "I'd like to take you all out to an R-rated movie, no lie!"

It had to be Jerome. I turned around. There was Jerome, standing on his crutches in the doorway, with Trevor and Brad.

Brad. Just seeing him made my heart turn over.

"You're only ten, you can't go to R-rated movies," Kimber reminded him.

"Ha," Jerome said. "I'm twenty-five. My growth has just been stunted because I smoke too many cigarettes."

Deena giggled. "You don't smoke cigarettes."

"I do, too, woman," Jerome insisted. "I smoke maybe seven, eight packs of cigarettes a day!"

"Jerome, did you see me cheer?" Heidi asked her hero.

"You were fierce, little mamma," Jerome assured her. He turned to Trevor and Brad. "Wasn't she fierce?"

"Fierce," they agreed, grinning at the little girl.

"Hi, Trevor," Dawn McKnight called, giving him a sexy look. It was very obnoxious.

"Hey," he said casually. "Don't let us interrupt you."

"You could never interrupt," she said in a teasing voice.

"Ooooooo!" the little girls tittered.

"Hey, do you love him?" Deena asked boldly.

"Maybe," Dawn said saucily.

"Ooooooooo!" all the little girls screamed, then they laughed hysterically.

"We're gonna show you guys one more cheer," Krystal said. "This is the hardest one we do. It's called 'Jump Back.'" She looked around at the other cheerleaders, who got into formation. "Ready? Let's go!"

"OUR GUYS ARE THE TOUGHEST,
WE CAN'T BE BEAT.
SO JUMP BACK, NOW,

YOU'RE GONNA TASTE DEFEAT.
HEY, JUMP BACK! JUMP BACK!
JUMP BACK!"
IT'S THE HOPE ATTACK,
SO JUMP BACK!"

The cheerleaders did an intricate hip-hop dance, where they jumped backward and did legovers every time they yelled "jump back." I was really impressed.

Everyone applauded at the end. Then Rachel and some other nurses brought in cookies, cupcakes, and juice. When the little girls had finally moved away from Krystal, I walked over to her.

"You are really great," I told her.

"Thanks," she said coolly.

"So, how long did it take you to learn to do cheers?"

She shrugged. "I don't know. I just have a talent for it, I guess."

Brad walked over to us, that incredibly cute, shy grin of his on his face. "Hi," he said.

I could actually *see* Krystal's guy radar go off. "Well, hi," she said. "Who are you?"

"Brad Kennedy," he said.

"Hi, Brad Kennedy," Krystal said. "I'm Krystal Franklin. You don't go to Hope Middle School, do you?"

"No," Brad said. "I go to a private school."

"If you went to Hope, I'd remember," she said flirtatiously.

"You guys were great," Brad said.

"Thanks," Krystal replied. "We've won the Michigan State Middle School Cheerleading Finals for two years in a row."

"Great," Brad said.

I did not like the way this conversation was going at all. Mainly because it felt like I didn't exist.

"Listen, we really want to thank you for coming to the hospital and doing this exhibition," I said in a loud voice, mostly just so I could get into the conversation.

"Oh, sure," Krystal said. "These poor kids." She looked over at Marissa, who was talking with Cindy, Veronica, and Trevor. "That little girl—what's her name again?"

"Marissa," Brad said.

"Yeah," Krystal said, fiddling with the little pearl earring in her left ear. "I feel so sorry for her. I mean, the kid is like something out of a horror movie, you know?"

"She was in a fire—" Brad began.

"Drag," Krystal commented with a shudder of revulsion. "If it was me I would want to, like, kill myself. Wouldn't you?"

"No," Brad said bluntly.

Krystal grinned and looked up at him from under her very thick eyelashes. "But you're so cute! It would be terrible if anything happened to *your* face!"

As Cindy would say, get me the hurl bag.

Brad blushed, but I could tell he was really flattered.

"Excuse me a minute," I said. "I need to go talk to Cindy and Veronica." I was hoping Brad would follow me, but he didn't. He just stood there with Krystal. It seemed like they barely acknowledged I was leaving.

"Help!" I hissed to Veronica, since Cindy was talking with Marissa. "Krystal is practically sucking face with Brad!"

Veronica looked over at her cousin. "It looks like they're just having a conversation."

"Some conversation," I lamented. "She's really, really flirting with him!"

"He won't fall for that," Veronica assured me. "Brad is very mature. I think it's because he's been so sick—"

"Sick with what?" I asked.

"He has to tell you himself," Veronica said.

I groaned. "Look, you already told me it

was a heart thing. Why does everyone act like it's some big secret? He looks healthy to me."

Veronica just shrugged.

Then a terrible thought occurred to me, and I grabbed her arm. "It's not AIDS, is it?"

"No," Veronica said firmly. "It isn't."

"Are you sure?"

"Positive," she said. "It's not that it's a big secret, it's just that—"

"Oh, no, she's touching him," I said, watching Krystal and Brad. Her hand was on his arm, and she was looking up at him and laughing. "She's actually touching him!"

I was not going to stand by and watch her try to get Brad away from me. No way. I quickly excused myself from Veronica, then I marched back over to Krystal and Brad.

"Hi!" I said brightly. "Long time no see!"

"Oh, hi, Deena," Krystal said.

"It's Tina," I corrected her. "Deena is over there. She's six years old and she's not Asian."

"Oh, are you Asian?" Krystal asked, then she cracked up as if that was the funniest joke in the world.

"Attention, attention, everyone!" Rachel

cried, banging a spoon against a glass. "How about a round of applause for our guests today, the Hope Middle School Cheerleaders!"

Everyone applauded. Krystal bobbed her head in acknowledgment, sort of like royalty.

"And I want to remind everyone that the Sixth Annual Hope Hospital Carnival is next Saturday!" Rachel continued. "It's a carnival to raise money for our pediatric unit, and it's going to be really super! We want to extend an invitation to all our new cheerleading friends to come to our carnival!"

Krystal turned to Brad. "A carnival! That sounds like fun."

"Yeah, it does," Brad agreed. "And it's for a great cause."

Krystal took Brad's arm again. "So, let me ask you a question, Brad Kennedy," she said. "How would you like to go to the carnival with me?"

Chapter 5

No, no, no, no. It couldn't be happening, but it was! Krystal Franklin, head cheerleader, had just asked Brad out! Right in front of my face!

I just stood there like a total idiot. I didn't know what to say or do. I wanted to punch her lights out, but of course I couldn't do that.

I held my breath and looked at the floor, waiting to hear Brad say how much he'd love to go to the carnival with the cute head cheerleader from Hope Middle School.

"Sorry, I can't," Brad said. "I'm going with Tina."

I looked up. Had he really said what I thought he'd said, or had I just wished it?

Krystal looked at me, shock written all over her face. "You're going with *her*?" she asked incredulously.

"Yep," Brad said. "At least I hope I am. I haven't asked her yet." He turned to me. "Tina, will you go to the carnival with me?"

"I'd love to," I replied. I could feel my cheeks stretching, my smile was so wide.

"I'm kind of...surprised," Krystal said. "No offense or anything."

Have you ever noticed that when people say "no offense" they always mean just the opposite?

"Gee, no offense taken," I said innocently.

"I mean, you're not even American," she added, wrinkling her nose.

"Well, since I was born in San Francisco, I think that makes me American—not that it matters," I told her in an even voice.

"But you're Asian," she pointed out. "You said so yourself!"

"Asian-American," I explained. "And unless you're an American Indian, your ancestors came from somewhere else, too."

Brad smiled at that. I smiled, too.

"Gee, thanks for the social studies lesson," Krystal said sarcastically. She looked from Brad to me. "So, are you two, like, a couple?"

"We're friends," Brad said.

"Yeah, but you're not boyfriend and girlfriend, right?" she asked.

"We're working on it," I said boldly. Then I did a really nervy thing. I reached for Brad's hand.

And he took it.

"Oh, how cute," Krystal said, venom dripping from her voice. She narrowed her eyes at me. "I won't forget this, Deena."

"Tina," I corrected her gleefully. "Tina Wu."

"Whatever!" she hissed, and stomped off.

"That was so fabulous!" I shrieked.

"She's a bigot and a snob," Brad said.

"You really want me to go to the carnival with you?" I asked him.

"Yeah," he said. "I'm sorry I asked you in front of her. It's just that girls like her really tick me off..."

"Me too," I agreed.

We stood there, smiling at each other, and I was the happiest girl on earth.

Because Brad Kennedy was still holding my hand.

* * *

"You guys, I had the greatest time today," I told Veronica and Cindy.

It was around seven o'clock that evening, and we were all over at Cindy's house, sitting on her front porch. We had just polished off the pizza her dad had ordered for dinner. I sat in a wicker rocking chair and stared blissfully up at the stars.

"It's very cool about you and Brad," Cindy said. Of course I had already told her and Veronica everything that had happened that afternoon.

"I'm happy for you," Veronica added. "You two make a wonderful couple."

"Couple!" I cried. "I *love* the sound of that word!"

"Lucky you," Cindy said with a sigh. "I'll probably never even *have* a boyfriend."

"Would someone please tell me what is so important about having a boyfriend?" Veronica asked.

"It just is," I said.

"And I'll never have one," Cindy added glumly.

"Of course you will," Veronica insisted.

"Not one I want," Cindy said pointedly.

We all knew who she was talking about.

"My prediction is that you and Trevor end up together," Veronica said.

"In my dreams," Cindy scoffed. She picked up a little stone and tossed it out on the grass. "Can I ask you guys a question?"

"Sure," I said.

"Have you ever been kissed?" Cindy asked.

Veronica smiled wickedly. "Kids start young in New York."

"I thought you told me you didn't have a boyfriend back there because you were so busy with ballet."

"Right," Veronica said. "But a guy doesn't have to be your boyfriend for you to kiss him."

"I never thought about that," I marveled. "I guess that's true. But it's so much more fun if you're totally in love..." Like I am with Brad, I thought to myself. Maybe he'll kiss me at the carnival. That would be so incredible. I closed my eyes blissfully and thought about what it would be like to kiss Brad Kennedy.

"So how many boys have you kissed?" Cindy asked Veronica.

"Four," Veronica said.

I opened my eyes. "Four?"

"Four?" Cindy echoed incredulously. "And none of them was even your boyfriend?"

Veronica shrugged. "I like to kiss. And I didn't want a boyfriend."

"Well, you've kissed four more boys than I've kissed," Cindy said gloomily. "I'm socially retarded." She looked over at me. "So have you been kissed?"

"Sure," I replied. "When I was in third grade this little boy in my class used to grab me and kiss me in the hall, and—"

"That's not exactly what I meant," Cindy said dryly.

"I knew that," I told her with a laugh. "Actually, I had a boyfriend last year in seventh grade."

"Where did you meet him, since you don't go to school?" Veronica asked.

"Church," I replied. "We used to sneak out of the service and kiss in the little kids' playground. My grandmother would have boiled me in oil if she knew."

"So what happened to him?" Cindy asked, reaching for another stone to throw out at the lawn.

"He moved to Ann Arbor," I explained. "But anyway, I wouldn't have stayed with him. He was cute and nice but really dumb and kind of boring. I was just so desperate for a boyfriend..."

"I don't know why girls think they have to have a boyfriend," Veronica said. "It's stupid."

"You only say that because you could probably get any guy on the planet," I said.

"I don't want just any boyfriend," Cindy pointed out. "I want one certain guy..." Her voice trailed off.

"Hi, kiddies," Clark said, bounding out of the house. "Cin, I'm going to Melanie's."

"Did you tell Dad you're taking the car?" Cindy asked him.

"He's on the phone," Clark said. "You tell him." He whistled and walked toward the car.

"He's such a brat," Cindy muttered.

"A cute brat," I said, watching him get into the Winterses' family car.

"He isn't cute, he's obnoxious," Cindy said. "And he's so shallow. His girlfriend Melanie is, like, a total airhead, but she's cute so he goes out with her."

I stared up at the stars, and a vision of Marissa's face came into my mind. "You know," I said softly, "we worry about being cute, but think of what someone like Marissa must go through."

"Would you want to live if you looked like that?" Cindy asked us.

"Of course I would," Veronica said. "Beauty isn't important and it doesn't last."

"That's easy for you to say," Cindy said.

"You're beautiful." She turned to me. I could just make out her features by the dim porch light. "Would you want to live, Tina?"

I thought about that a moment. I knew I should say that I'd want to live, that how a person looks isn't that important. But then I thought of all those kids staring at Marissa with horror, of what it would be like to not be able to go to the mall or something without everyone staring at you and pointing at you. And then I thought about Brad. Would Brad ever want to kiss me if I looked like Marissa? Would I really want to live like that?

"I don't know," I told Cindy honestly. "I really don't know."

"Okey-dokey, this is super!" Rachel Dander said, tapping her pencil on the list she'd just made.

It was Wednesday night, and we were at the final organizational meeting for the carnival. Between the hospital staff and the volunteers there were about thirty people at the meeting. Veronica and Cindy were, of course, at the meeting with me. Trevor was sitting between the two of them.

And Brad was sitting next to me.

"So, everyone has their assignment for Saturday," Rachel chirped. "I just want to say I think this is going to be the best carnival we've ever had!"

Cindy's dad, Dr. Dan, stood up and put his arm around Rachel. "How about a round of applause for Rachel for all the great work she's doing?"

Everyone applauded, and Rachel actually curtsied. I shot Cindy a significant look that said "This is the woman your father is secretly dating." Cindy didn't look any too thrilled about it, I can tell you that.

The meeting broke up, and Brad and I wandered over to the refreshment table to get some lemonade.

"I can't believe Rachel is planning to dress up in her Tinker Bell costume for the entire carnival," I told Brad with a laugh.

"And sprinkle fairy dust on people who make extra contributions to the pediatric wing," he added. "She's kind of scary."

"The little kids like her," I said, reaching for a chocolate chip cookie. "But I can't believe that Dr. Dan is actually going out with her."

"Is he?" Brad asked with surprise.

"Yep," I confirmed. I reached for another cookie. They were great. "She's madly in love with him. She told Virgin-for-Life Nurse Virginia Overton in the nurses' lounge a few days ago. It's certainly not my fault if they left the door open and I could hear every word they said to each other."

Brad laughed. "You should start your own hospital gossip column."

"That's not a bad idea!" I replied.

"Hey, you want to go look in at Marissa?" Brad suggested.

"I'm sure she's asleep," I said. Marissa's surgery had been the day before. The doctors told us it had gone really well. But her face was wrapped in bandages and she was on heavy pain medications that made her sleep most of the time.

"We could just peek into the room," Brad said. "She'll be so happy if she's awake."

I smiled at him. What a nice guy.

"Okay," I agreed.

We walked down to Marissa's room and carefully opened her door. She was sound asleep. The bandages wound around the center of her face, making her look kind of like a mummy.

"I wonder what she'll look like when those bandages come off," Brad whispered.

"She'll have a nose, at least," I whispered back. We shut the door and stood in the hallway. "But she told me she has to have, like, six different surgeries or something, before it's all done."

Brad nodded sadly. "And even then she won't look like she did before the fire."

"How do you know?" I asked with surprise.

"Well, she told me. She's really an incredible little girl," he said. "I've been spending a lot of time hanging out with her."

"You didn't tell me that." I leaned against the wall and put my hands behind my waist.

Brad shrugged. Then he reached into his back pocket and pulled a small photograph out of his wallet, which he handed to me.

It was Marissa at about age seven, clearly before the fire.

"She gave me that," Brad said.

"She was so cute," I exclaimed, staring at the photo of a smiling little girl wheeling a new bike. I handed the photo back to him. "What happened with the fire, did she tell you?"

He put the photo back in his wallet. "Marissa's cousin was playing with matches, and the house caught on fire," Brad told me. "Marissa was in the back bedroom asleep because she had the flu. The firefighters barely got her out. She almost died."

"Wow," I breathed. It was so terrible. I just didn't know what to say. "How come we never see her parents visit her here?"

"They're dead," Brad said. "She lives with her aunt and uncle. Dr. Dan told me he thinks they feel so guilty, because it was their son playing with the matches that started the fire, that they don't come to the hospital very often."

"That is so awful," I said. I couldn't even imagine how terrible that would be. My family might drive me crazy, but they certainly were always there for me. In fact, I had to practically beg them to not camp out at the hospital every time I was admitted. If it was up to my grandmother, she'd sleep at the foot of my bed. She doesn't believe anyone can possibly take care of me the way she can.

I looked at Brad again. "I wonder why Marissa told you so much more than she told us," I mused.

Maybe because I've been here as a patient all this time, like her," Brad said.

"Well, I'm a patient here often enough, myself," I pointed out.

"Yeah, but she didn't meet you as another patient. She met you as one of three best friends that just hang out here being nice to people."

"I see your point," I said.

"Want to go for a walk?" Brad asked me.

"We just did," I said with a laugh.

"I mean outside."

"Sure," I agreed. We walked past the pediatric nurses' station, where I told Rachel to let Cindy and Veronica know where I was, then we went outside and slowly walked across the grassy park area on the side of the hospital.

"I'm getting out tomorrow," Brad said quietly. He sat down on a redwood picnic table and put his feet on the bench.

"That's fantastic!" I cried. I sat down next to him. Close but not too close, if you know what I mean. I looked at him out of the corner of my eyes. "Brad?"

"Hmmm?"

"I really wish you'd tell me what's wrong with you," I said quietly.

"I don't like to talk about it very much," he mumbled, staring down at his hands.

"But you know all about me having lupus," I said. "It's not like I don't know what it's like to be sick a lot."

"Yeah," Brad said.

Silence.

"So?" I prompted.

Brad picked up a leaf and slowly rolled it in his fingers. "It's called atrial septal defect," he finally said in a low voice.

"What is that?"

"It's my heart," he said quietly. "I was born with a hole in my heart."

"You were..." I didn't know what to say. "Does it hurt?"

"Not unless I want to actually do anything," he said bitterly. "I can't run, I can't do sports, I can't even dance."

"So...can they fix it?" I asked him.

"They're trying to," Brad said. "It's been getting a lot worse, the last few years. So they tried this thing where they stuck a thin tube in my arm and threaded it up to my heart to try and patch the hole."

"Did it work?"

Brad threw the leaf to the ground. "Nope."

"So now what happens?" I asked in a whispery voice.

"Well, that's what they've been trying to figure out," Brad said. "But I think I'm probably going to have to have open heart surgery."

A shiver ran up my spine. "I reached for Brad's hand. "That's scary."

He just nodded and squeezed my hand hard. "I don't want to do it. I hate the idea of someone messing with my heart."

"Well, what if you don't have the surgery?" I asked.

He was silent for a minute, then he looked at me. "If I don't have the surgery," he said, "I die."

Chapter 6

"You look fabulous," I told Marissa Saturday morning as I straightened the red bow I had just put in her hair. It matched the red sweater that we'd picked out for her.

I'd dressed carefully myself. It was, after all, my first official date with Brad. Not that my grandparents or my parents knew I had an official date. Since I am not allowed to officially date until I'm sixteen, they would have officially killed me.

I wore a black pleated miniskirt and black tights, with a red and black checked flannel shirt and suspenders. In addition to my usual mascara and lip gloss (which I always put on *after* I leave my house or I wouldn't be let out the door), I had put on a tiny bit of blush.

Cindy had on jeans, per usual, and a T-shirt underneath a denim shirt. Veronica had on black jeans and a white cotton shirt with black embroidery. Her hair was loose except for a tiny brain down one side, tied at the bottom with the smallest of black ribbons.

"Red is clearly your color," Veronica told her, straightening the collar of Marissa's sweater.

"Thanks," Marissa managed. Her voice sounded even more muffled than before since her nose was encased in bandages.

"Okay, are you ready to go to this bash?" Cindy asked her.

Marissa nodded eagerly. "Is Heidi coming?"

"Heidi has a fever today," Cindy explained. "The doctor said she has to stay in bed."

"She must be so mad," Marissa said in her funny voice.

"She is," Veronica agreed. "But we'll bring her prizes later, okay?"

"Okay," Marissa agreed.

"Your chariot, Madame," I said, bowing low.

We helped her go from the bed to the wheelchair. She was still kind of weak and woozy from her surgery, and she was still taking a lot of pain medication.

"Where's Brad?" Marissa asked, as we wheeled her into the hallway.

"Right here," Brad said, since he and Trevor had been waiting right outside her door. "We wanted to give you private time to get beautiful."

"A beautiful mummy!" Marissa said with a muffled laugh.

"World's most beautiful mummy," Trevor told her with a grin. "And the mummy part is strictly temporary."

"I'll take Marissa," Veronica said quickly, taking the handles of Marissa's wheelchair. "The four of you can go have fun."

"We can all hang out together," Cindy protested, even though I knew deep down inside she was probably thrilled to have a chance to be alone with Trevor.

"No, Marissa and I have things to discuss," Veronica said. "We'll see you later."

"Bye!" Marissa said as Veronica pushed her toward the kids' lounge.

I looked at my watch. "Well, I have exactly a half hour of freedom before I have to report to the pie-throwing booth."

"Why did you ever volunteer to let people throw pies at you?" Cindy asked me as we walked slowly toward the lounge.

"Temporary insanity," I said with a laugh. "Anyway, your dad told me the throwers have to stand so far away that last year only two people actually got hit at the pie booth all day. I figure I'm safe for an hour."

"Just pray no one with great aim shows up," Trevor said.

"Look at it this way," I replied, "I am a wonderful human being. It costs five tickets for the pie booth, and if you win you get one of those giant stuffed animals. Since hardly anyone ever wins, I'll be responsible for making a ton of money for the hospital!"

"Wow, it's already hopping," Brad said as we entered the lounge.

There were booths everywhere, and loud music was playing over a speaker system. The room was filled with people of all ages, running around, shouting, laughing, and trying their luck at the various booths. Dr. Dan was dressed as a clown, and he was juggling in a ring in the center of the room. Rachel, also known as Tinker Bell, was standing by him with a rapturous look on her face.

"Aren't they darling together?" I teased Cindy.

"Please," she snorted. "You know what she did last night? I picked up the phone to call you, and Dad was already on the other extension. He was talking to *her*. So before I could hang up, I hear her singing to him in this dopey voice: 'I love you a bushel and a peck.'"

"Lame!" Trevor said with a laugh.

"Seriously," Brad agreed.

"Do I hear wedding bells?" I asked, cupping my hand to my ear.

"I'll run away from home first," Cindy said darkly.

"Hey, forget Tinker Bell," Trevor told her. "Let's go get some junk food. I see a chili dog booth over there." He reached for Cindy's hand and they took off.

"Wow, this is so cool!" I exclaimed. "Cindy is going to be in heaven!"

"Why?" Brad asked.

We walked by a pitch-the-penny-in-the-bottle booth and a line of people waiting to have their caricature drawn by none other than Virgin-for-Life Nurse Virginia Overton.

"Because she's in love with Trevor," I explained. "You must know that."

"Oh, yeah," Brad said. "He likes her, too."

"Really?" I asked, whirling around to face him. "He told you?"

"Hey, I'm not breaking any guy confidences here," Brad said with a grin.

"What, he told you stuff about her in confidence?" I asked eagerly. "You have to tell me!"

"No, I don't," Brad said. "If Cindy told you something in confidence, I wouldn't expect you to tell me. It would be really immature."

"True," I said with a sigh. "But sometimes being mature is so awful!"

Brad laughed and lightly touched my back with his right hand. It was almost-sort-of like he was putting his arm around me. "Want a cotton candy?"

"Sure!" I said. "I have to eat all the sugar I can when I'm out in the world. My grandmother thinks white sugar is the downfall of humankind."

"Two cotton candies, please," Brad told the guy manning the cotton candy machine.

He handed me one and I bit into the spun sugar. "Mmmm, I love this!"

"It's great," Brad agreed, pulling off a handful.

"I was thinking..." I said slowly, pulling off some more spun sugar.

"Yeah?"

"About what you told me yesterday," I said. "I asked Veronica what was wrong with you, back when you wouldn't tell me anything. And she said it was your heart—"

"So why did you keep pestering me?" Brad asked.

"Well, because that's all she'd say," I explained. "And she also told me that whatever was wrong with your heart wasn't so serious."

Brad looked away. "It didn't used to be. It's gotten worse."

"Meaning she doesn't know about the surgery thing," I said.

"Yeah."

I plucked off another wad of cotton candy. "So...would you...I mean...it sounds like you really need to have this surgery, right?"

Brad shrugged. "Doctors aren't right all the time, you know."

"I know," I agreed. "But if they're right this time...then...well, you'll have the surgery, right?"

"Believe it or not, I don't get a say in it," Brad said bitterly. "My parents decide."

"Don't they care what you want?" I asked with surprise.

Brad looked at me. "If your parents

thought you needed surgery to save your life, and you didn't want to do it, would they care what you wanted?"

"No," I replied. "They would be sure that they knew better."

"Welcome to being a kid—which is what they think we are," Brad said, an edge to his voice. "We don't get any say in our own lives."

"Well, well, well, look who's here," a nasty voice sing-songed. It was Krystal Franklin, standing right in front of us. Dawn McKnight was with her. "It's Deena, right?" she asked me.

"Tina," I corrected her.

"Oh, yeah," Krystal said. She looked over at Brad. "Hi, Brad."

"Hi," he said.

"Slumming, I see," she told him.

"If that's supposed to be funny, I don't get it," Brad said bluntly.

Krystal and Dawn exchanged nasty looks. "I just mean that you can do better than Deena, here."

Brad put his arm around me. "It's Tina," he said, "and we're kind of busy..."

"Look, I'm not being mean," Krystal said. "I'm just trying to tell you the truth."

I looked her straight in the eye. "I don't

understand you. You don't know me and I don't know you. I never did anything to you. So why are you being so nasty to me?"

"Let me put it this way," Krystal said, shaking some hair off her face. "I can get any guy I want. I'm not bragging, it's just the way it is. And I think it's a joke if someone like you thinks that you can stop me."

Brad laughed. "I'm really flattered if you're fighting over me—"

"Just what do you mean by 'someone like me'?" I asked Krystal heatedly. "You mean because I'm Asian?"

"Asian-*American,*" Krystal taunted me. Dawn laughed. "And also," Krystal continued, "you're kind of chubby, and you're not very cute."

"Well, that's a matter of opinion," I said with dignity, even though I felt totally embarrassed. "I happen to think I'm darling."

"Maybe in Japan or something, you are!" Krystal exclaimed. This cracked Dawn up all over again.

"I'll tell you what you are," Brad said, looking right at Krystal. "You're a bigot. And no matter how cute you are on the outside, you're not very cute on the inside, which gives you a case of the serious uglies in my book." He turned to me and took my hand. "Come on, Tina."

"Big deal," Krystal called after us. "He's not that fine, you know! And I could get him if I really wanted to!"

"You were great," I told Brad as we hurried away from Krystal and Dawn. I could feel my face burning with humiliation.

"So were you," Brad said. He gave me a sidelong look. "Do you have to put up with junk like that very often?"

I shook my head no. "It's only happened once or twice in my whole life. I can't understand it. Does she just hate me because I don't look like her and her friends?"

"Something like that, I guess," Brad said.

I looked at my watch. "Oh, gosh, I have to get to the pie booth. I'm five minutes late already."

"Good luck!" Brad said. "I'll meet you over there in an hour."

"Hopefully I won't have any pie on my face!" I told him, and I raced across the lounge. "Hi!" I exclaimed to Brenda Shirley, a nurse's aide who was running the pie booth. I'm really sorry I'm late!"

"No prob," Brenda said. "No one has hit Dr. Maxwell anyway."

"And I'm glad to quit while I'm ahead!" Dr.

Maxwell said, pulling his head out of the cardboard cutout of a bodybuilder.

"Thanks, Dr. Maxwell," Brenda said. "You were great."

Dr. Maxwell is an oncologist, meaning that he works with cancer patients. He treats a lot of the kids, like Brianna and Jerome. He's got curly red hair and a red beard. He's very tall and kind of barrel-chested, and he's pretty overweight, too. But somehow he's really cute, anyway. Dr. Maxwell is married and has three kids, and Virgin-for-Life Nurse Virginia Overton has the world's hugest crush on him.

Like I said, I know everything that goes on at the hospital.

"It was fun," the doctor said. He gave me a friendly wink. "Good luck in there."

"Just stick your head in the hole over the bodybuilder," Brenda instructed me. "The louder and more obnoxious you are, the more tickets we'll sell." She leaned close to me. "And just between you and me," she whispered, "when they stand behind that line, you're next to impossible to hit."

"Gotcha," I said as I fitted my head through the hole. "Step right up, step right up!" I called to the crowd. "No one can hit me with a pie! I dare ya! I double dare ya!"

"Hit the bodybuilder with a pie and win a huge stuffed animal!" Brenda called. "All you have to do is stand behind that line and hit her in the face with this whipped cream pie!"

"Come on, everybody!" I yelled. I was starting to have fun. It's not often you get permission to be totally obnoxious. "No one can hit me! You're all chicken! Brawk! Brawk!" I cackled, doing my best chicken imitation.

I was looking around the room, trying to see if I could locate my friends, when I heard an all too familiar female voice say, "Five tickets, please."

Krystal Franklin. With some guy I had never seen before who was approximately the size of a small truck. He had beady little eyes, a crew cut that showed his scalp, and no neck. And Krystal was handing the pie to him.

Uh-oh.

"Hi, there, Deena," she said in a most malicious voice. "You are one dead chicken."

"You have to stand behind the line," Brenda said quickly. She pointed to the line on the floor.

"Sure thing," the guy said. He hefted the pie in his hand and gave me a smile like something out of a horror movie. "This one's for you, Krystal," the guy said.

"Thanks, Duke," Krystal said.

"No prob," Duke mumbled, eyeing me carefully.

I gulped hard. "Uh, no need to take your aggressions out on little ole me," I squeaked.

"Nail her, Duke," Krystal said.

He pulled his arm back and heaved that pie at me as hard as he could.

I squeezed my eyes shut and prepared for my doom.

Nothing happened. I opened my eyes.

"Ha, missed!" Brenda crowed. Then she realized she wasn't supposed to gloat over him missing the target, namely me. "I mean, gee, too bad," she corrected herself. "Okay, who's next? Five tickets buys you a pie!"

"Too bad, Duke!" I yelled, giddy with relief. "Better luck next time, big guy!"

"Here's twenty more tickets," Krystal said, handing the rest of her tickets to Brenda. "Duke will take the next four pies."

"But—but you can only try once," Brenda improvised.

"There's no sign that says that," Krystal replied snottily. She reached for Duke's arm. "Duke, make me proud."

"Will do, Krystal," Duke agreed. He hurled another pie at me.

And missed.

A crowd began to form. Brad was standing next to Veronica and Marissa. Cindy was on the other side with Trevor. I put my hand through the head hole in the cardboard cutout and waggled my fingers at Brad.

"Hit her this time!" Krystal hissed to Duke.

"No probs, Krystal," Duke said. He did a windup this time and let the pie fly.

And missed.

"Hey, this thing is fixed or something!" Duke bellowed.

"Maybe you just can't aim!" someone in the crowd called out good-naturedly.

"Aim this time," Krystal commanded, her eyes narrowing.

"Okay, I will," Duke assured her. "I got her this time."

He missed.

And missed again.

Now the crowd was laughing and cheering, all for me. Brad gave me a *V* for victory sign.

"This is my last pie," Duke told Krystal.

"I can see that," she seethed through clenched teeth. "And if you miss this time, I'm not letting you drive me home!"

"Miss, miss, miss, miss!" the crowd began to chant.

I joined in. "Miss, miss, miss, miss! You couldn't hit the side of a barn!" I yelled, thoroughly enjoying myself.

Duke went for the windup. He pulled back, and then, quick as a flash, he took a huge step over the line on the floor. And heaved the pie at me full-force.

Splat. Bull's-eye. Whipped cream was in my eyes and my hair. I inhaled out of surprise and snorted it up into my nose and mouth.

"Ha! Gotcha!" Duke yelled triumphantly.

"That doesn't count!" Brenda yelled. "You went way over the line!"

"Cheater," someone called. "You cheated, man!"

"I'm sorry, but you can't win the giant stuffed bear because you were way too close to the target," Brenda told Duke. Duke's face fell.

"So?" Krystal replied snottily. "I didn't want the stupid stuffed animal, anyway." She grinned at me in a ugly way. I could barely make her out through the whipped cream gunked in my eyes. "I got what I wanted. Let's go, Duke."

"Are you okay?" Veronica asked me, wheeling Marissa over to me. Cindy was close behind with a towel, which she handed to me.

I pulled my head out of the cardboard hole and began to wipe the gunk off my face. "He threw that hard," I said.

"He's a Neanderthal," Cindy said. "I know

him. Duke Denny. He's on the football team at Hope High. They call him Ding-Dong Duke because he's so stupid."

"Is Krystal going out with him?" I asked as I tried to wipe the whipped cream out of my ears.

"I doubt it," Cindy said. "He's, like, sixteen years old! I think she just saw him here and told him he could drive her home if he hit you with a pie."

"In other words she used him," Veronica said.

"Krystal hates my guts," I told them. "You should have heard her ragging on me before."

"She can be really nice or really cruel," Cindy explained. "I've seen her be really mean to some of the nerdy kids at school..."

"And to Marilee," Veronica reminded Cindy. "Marilee is the only black girl in our class, and Krystal is horrible to her."

"It's really weird," I said, shaking my head, "to have someone hate me who doesn't even know me..."

"Ignore her," Marissa said in her muffled voice. "That's what I try to do when people hate me because of how I look."

I smiled and carefully gave Marissa a

hug. "That's really good advice."

"I just hate bigots," Veronica said, narrowing her eyes.

"I hate cheaters," Marissa said.

"Me too," Cindy said vehemently. "He was standing so close to you when he hit you—it was totally unfair."

"Hi," Brad said, walking over with Trevor. "I brought you a glass of water." He handed it to me.

"Should I drink it or pour it on myself?" I asked. I dipped the towel into the water and tried to wash my face.

"Hi," Brenda said, walking over to us. "I'm really sorry about that. He cheated."

"It's not your fault," I told her. "Anyway, I'm okay."

"You can go get cleaned up if you want," Brenda said. "Dr. Dan is coming on for his shift in ten minutes, anyway."

"My dad's doing it?" Cindy asked with surprise.

Brenda nodded. "And Rachel's taking over for me."

"I am so gunky," I said, pulling my shirt away from me. The pie had hit me with such force that the whipped cream had gotten into the neckline of my shirt. "I have to change."

"You can wear something of mine," Marissa offered.

"Thanks," I said, "but everything of yours would be too small for me."

"I have a really big University of Michigan sweatshirt," she told me. "It fits anybody."

"Okay," I said with a grin. "Thanks." I turned to Brad. "I'll be right back."

He smiled at me. "You're a very cool girl, Tina."

"Thanks," I said, suddenly feeling shy.

"I'll wait here with Brad," Trevor said.

Veronica wheeled Marissa, and we were hurrying toward Marissa's room when we ran into Krystal and Dawn, who were on their way out the door.

"Well, hi there, Deena," Krystal jeered. "You looked really funny with whipped cream all over your face and mascara running down your cheeks."

"Your boyfriend cheated," I told her.

She shrugged. "He's not my boyfriend. And anyway, I got what I wanted." She smirked at Dawn, who smirked back.

"I don't know why you hate me so much," I said. It was hard for me to accept that someone could be so cruel to me, just because of what race I was or how I looked.

"Oh, lighten up," Krystal said. "It was just a joke."

An old car with a noisy muffler pulled up, and someone honked the horn loudly. "Bye," Krystal said. "No hard feelings!" She and Dawn ran out to Duke, who had opened the car door from the inside for them.

"Amazing," Veronica said. "She thinks she can just do or say whatever she wants, and then after she hurts you she tells you to just forget the whole thing."

"Well, actually, she's right," I said. Everyone looked at me with surprise. "I mean I agree, let's forget the whole thing. I'm going to change and go back to the carnival and have a blast with Brad. And I don't intend to let Krystal Franklin stop me!"

I did have a blast. Brad and I spent the next two hours trying every single game. I even tried to pie Dr. Dan, just to see what it was like to be on the other side of things!

At the turtle race my turtle won two races in a row, and I won two giant stuffed turtles. I named one Jerome and the other Brad. Brad (the real one, not the turtle!) and I took Jerome (the turtle, not the real one!) in to Heidi, but she was asleep. We left

Jerome at the foot of her bed. After that we went for a walk, back to the picnic area on the side of the hospital.

"That thing doesn't look anything like me!" Brad said, looking at my new stuffed turtle.

"I know," I agreed, "but now I can hug one Brad at night before I go to sleep."

As soon as those words popped out of my mouth, I realized how racy they sounded, but it was too late to take them back. I wasn't sure how Brad would take it.

But then he reached for my hand.

Bliss.

"So, I'm going back to school on Monday," he told me.

"I wish I went to school," I said wistfully, "instead of to the garage."

"My school's pretty good," Brad said. "I've got a great art teacher."

"I'm jealous," I told him.

We walked over to the picnic table and sat down. It was starting to get cold, and I hugged my new stuffed turtle Brad to me for warmth.

"So...my school is having a dance in a couple of weeks," Brad said casually.

My heart beat faster. Was he about to invite me? Was that really possible?

"Uh-huh," I said, hugging my turtle.

"I can't fast dance because of my heart," he said.

I smiled at him. "I'm a crummy dancer, myself."

He smiled back. "So, does that mean that you wouldn't mind if we didn't fast dance? I can slow dance."

"Are you...inviting me to your dance?" I asked, half holding my breath.

"Yeah," he said softly.

"I'd love to go!" I cried happily. I knew it wasn't supposed to be cool to let a guy know how happy you were if he asked you out, but I didn't care.

Brad put his arm around me and gave me a quick hug. "That's great. That's really great!"

I decided not to think about what my parents or my grandparents would say about me having a date to a dance with Brad. They would say no, that was for sure, which meant I had to find a way to either convince them or sneak out of the house.

Because no way was I going to miss that dance. No way.

"It's getting cold out," I said, shivering a little. Of course I wasn't really that cold. I just wanted him to hold me closer.

And he did. "Better?" he asked.

"Much," I said happily. I kind of put my head down on his shoulder. And then I could feel it—that moment when he decided he was going to kiss me.

Oh my gosh, Brad Kennedy was going to kiss me.

He moved a little away from me so that he could see my face. Then he moved closer. I closed my eyes just before his lips touched mine, and then—

"Tina! Tina!" It was Cindy, running toward us, sounding frantic.

Brad and I pulled quickly apart. I was not thrilled to see her.

"What?" I said.

"It's Krystal," she said, breathing hard.

"What about her?" I asked irritably. Krystal Franklin was the last person I wanted to think about while Brad was kissing me. I didn't care what horrible prank she'd pulled.

"Duke and Krystal were in a car accident," she gasped. "Someone just ran up from emergency and told me. Duke's bruised up, but Krystal got the worst of it. They're bringing her in in an ambulance now."

"How bad is it?" Brad asked.

"Bad," Cindy said. "They don't know if she's going to make it."

Chapter 8

"This is just so bizarre," I said, as we sat in the emergency room, waiting to see how Krystal was. "I mean, we were just talking to her a few hours ago..."

"Sometimes I hate this hospital," Cindy said under her breath.

I reached for her hand. I guessed that she was thinking about her mom, and Brianna, and Heidi, too. She began rocking her body back and forth, very slowly, holding on to her sides as if she was afraid to let go.

Brad and Trevor had gone home. Veronica, Cindy, and I were sitting together on one side of the room. A bunch of people

I didn't know were sitting on the other side with Dawn. Evidently Ding-Dong Duke had already dropped Dawn off before the accident.

"We don't have to stay here," Veronica said softly, touching Cindy on the shoulder. "I hope that Krystal pulls through, but it's not like she's a friend of ours."

Cindy stopped rocking and got up. "You're right," she said. "I can't even breathe in here." She looked over at me.

"I can't leave," I said in a low voice.

"Of course you can," Cindy said.

I shook my head no. "I know it's crazy, but I feel like if I sit here she'll be okay, and if I leave she'll..."

I wouldn't say the word *die.*

"You guys can go if you want," I said. "There's no reason we all have to stay here."

Cindy and Veronica looked at each other.

"We're staying with you," Cindy decided.

"Of course," Veronica added. She sat down next to me.

"I know you guys thinks I'm crazy," I said.

"Just a little," Cindy said.

"If you were hurt, Krystal would definitely not be sitting out here worrying about you," Veronica pointed out.

"I know," I agreed, twisting some hair around my finger. "But I know what it feels like to be a patient here. And I guess...I guess..." It was so hard for me to explain what I was feeling. "Once I got admitted," I said slowly, "and I was really, really sick, and I kept wishing I had a friend there..."

"Where were your friends?" Cindy asked.

"What friends?" I asked. "I'm home-schooled, remember?"

"Krystal isn't your friend," Veronica said.

"I know," I agreed. "I know I'm crazy."

Veronica nudged me with her shoulder. "You are crazy," she agreed. "And you are also a very, very good person."

Duke came out of the examining room, and was immediately surrounded by his parents and friends. His arm was in an ace bandage and there was a gash on his forehead, but other than that he looked okay.

I walked over to Duke. "What happened?"

"We got hit from behind on River Road," he told me. "I slowed down a little and some fool rammed into me, it wasn't my fault—"

"Your car is a junk heap," Dawn cried bitterly. "Your taillights don't work, so how could the person behind you know if you were slowing down?"

"It wasn't my fault," Duke insisted. "Anyway, I had my seat belt on. Ever since my Uncle Al got killed because he didn't wear a seat belt, I wear one. So I asked Krystal to put hers on, but she just laughed. So, when this guy hit us, she...she went through the windshield—"

"Oh, God," Dawn cried, clapping her hand over her mouth.

"I'm real sorry," Duke said. "I told her to wear her seat belt..."

Dawn turned away from him, sobbing hysterically. Her friends put their arms around her.

I walked back over to Veronica and Cindy and told them what had happened.

"But will she live?" Cindy whispered. "That's what I have to know..."

A youngish male doctor with curly brown hair came out and walked briskly over to Krystal's parents.

"I wish I could hear what he was saying," I muttered. I sidled over to them to see if I could eavesdrop.

"...she's going in and out of consciousness," the doctor was saying. "We suspect a concussion, though the head X-rays don't look too bad."

"So, she's going to be okay, isn't she?"

Krystal's mom asked anxiously.

"It's too soon to say for sure," the doctor said. "I think her chances are good."

"Thank God!" her mother cried, burying her head in her husband's chest. "I want to see my baby!"

"You should know, though," the doctor continued in a grave voice, "most of the impact was taken by her face."

"So what does that mean?" Krystal's father asked.

The doctor took a deep breath. "There's no nice way to put this. Her face is badly damaged. If she pulls through, she's going to need extensive plastic surgery—"

"Anything!" her mother cried. "My baby girl is beautiful!"

The doctor took another deep breath. "You need to know the truth so that you can help your daughter get through this," he said slowly. "She's going to be scarred and badly disfigured, but eventually—"

"What do you mean, disfigured?" Krystal's mother screamed.

"Please, try to control yourself," the doctor said. "She's going to need your help. I don't want you to be too upset when you go in to see her—"

"We want to see our daughter now!" Mr.

Franklin demanded imperiously.

"You need to listen to me first, sir," the doctor said in a steely voice. "Your daughter needs you to be strong now. If she's awake, just reassure her that she's going to be okay. And don't show your reaction to her face—"

"Why?" Krystal's mom asked fearfully.

"Because her face is so badly disfigured that you won't recognize her," the doctor said bluntly.

I gasped and took a few steps backward.

It was like Marissa. It was just like Marissa.

"Hey, pretty momma, how's that cheerleader girl doing?" Jerome asked me as he smoothly maneuvered his way across the kids' lounge. It was amazing how well he could get around on one leg.

It was the next day, and me, Cindy, and Veronica had just finished reading to Heidi, Deena, Marielle, and some of the other little kids. Heidi's fever was down, and she was feeling much better. She took her new stuffed turtle, Jerome, with her everywhere she went.

Marissa was sitting next to me, drawing my picture.

"She's going to live," Cindy said.

"That's good," Jerome said, taking a seat next to Veronica. "I heard her face got all messed up."

"That's what we heard, too," Veronica said.

"Does it hurt?" Heidi lisped around the thumb in her mouth. I noticed that lately she seemed to be kind of regressing and acting more babyish. Dr. Dan said it was because she was in pain so often and acting like a baby comforted her.

"I'm sure it does," I told Heidi.

"Sometimes I hurt," Marielle whispered, "because I have sickle-cell anemia."

"I know," I told her. "I wish you didn't."

"Me too," she said seriously.

"Diabetes doesn't hurt," Deena said. "I'm lucky."

Heidi took her thumb out of her mouth. "I miss Brianna."

"Me too," Deena said.

"Me three," I agreed, gulping hard.

"Yeah, sure," Jerome agreed, "but think about this, ladies. Brianna was in a whole lot of pain a lot of the time, right? So now she doesn't hurt anymore."

I really had to marvel at that kid. He came up with the most adult things.

"So?" Marielle said. "I'd rather hurt and be

alive." She scratched her knee with a skinny, shaking hand. "Am I gonna die?" she asked, looking at me.

I felt a moment of total panic. "I don't know," I said.

"Yeah, you're gonna die," Jerome told her. "What do you think, you're gonna be the only human on earth who lives forever?"

Marielle giggled. Trust Jerome to say just the right thing. I made a mental note to ask Dr. Dan what we should say if a kid asked us a question like that. I sure didn't know how to handle it.

"So, that cheerleader babe," Jerome said, changing the subject, "is her face messed up forever, or what?"

"I don't know," I told him. "I heard she's going to have to have a lot of plastic surgery."

"Like me," Marissa put in. "It's not so bad. You're asleep when they do it, and then you wake up and feel kind of sick, but then after a while you feel better." She erased something on her sketch pad. "This is the best drawing I've done of you yet, Tina."

"It's one major drag about her face," Jerome said. "She was one twentieth-century fox."

"What does that mean?" Heidi asked him.

"It means she was a babe," he explained with a wink, "like you."

Heidi giggled and hugged her stuffed turtle. "I'm not a baby!"

"Not a baby, woman," Jerome growled at her. "A babe. A fox. It means she's cute."

"I'm not," Heidi said sadly.

"Listen," Jerome told her, "I've dated two, three hundred girls, and I know cute when I see cute."

Heidi gave him a shy smile.

"So did you see her yet?" Jerome asked.

"Not yet," Veronica said. "She can't have any visitors for a while except for her immediate family."

"So, what happened?" Jerome asked.

"A car hit them from behind," I explained.

"Man, I'm gonna get the guy that did that," Jerome decided. "Me and my gang will ice the dude."

"Can she still be a cheerleader?" Deena wondered.

"I don't see why not," I replied. "Once she's healthy again and everything."

"No one wants a cheerleader with a messed up face," Marissa said as she sketched in the hair on her drawing.

"Cheerleading is based on talent," I said.

"You have to be athletic, and a good dancer—"

"And you have to be pretty," Marissa said simply. "I wanted to be a cheerleader more than anything in the world, but now I don't want to anymore."

"Why is that?" Veronica asked her, tenderly smoothing her fingers across Marissa's curls.

"Because if you want something with all your heart and it can never happen, your heart breaks," Marissa said simply.

She's right, I thought. She's totally right. I wonder if she was always this smart, or if somehow going through what she's gone through has made her grow up fast.

No one said anything for a while. Jerome wandered over toward the TV with Heidi. Marielle wheeled in alongside them. Some of the other kids went to a table to color. Finally Marissa finished her picture.

"There," she said, showing it to me. "What do you think?"

"I think you are one talented nine year old," I marveled. "Look at this, you guys!" I showed the drawing to Veronica and Cindy.

"It's fabulous!" Veronica said. "Really!"

Cindy was staring out the window.

"Hey, Cin, did you see this?" I asked her.

She didn't respond, she just kept staring out the window.

"Oh, Cinderella!" I singsonged.

"What?" she asked, turning her head. "Oh, yeah, it's good," she said absently, and then went back to staring out the window.

Marissa touched Cindy's hand. "Are you sad?"

"No, I'm okay," Cindy said.

"Sad about Krystal?" Marissa asked.

"She's not a friend of mine," Cindy said truthfully.

"But you're the one who invited her to come here and do cheerleading for us!" Marissa reminded her.

"I know," Cindy said. She sat down next to Marissa. "But really, we're not friends at school or anything."

"Why?" Marissa asked.

"Well," Cindy began thoughtfully, "I don't think that she and her friends are very nice a lot of the time. Sometimes they're mean to kids who aren't popular."

"I hate that," Veronica said.

"Me too," Marissa agreed. She doodled a design in the corner of her sketch pad. "Did you ever notice that if you're pretty people like you, even if you're not nice?"

"Not always," Veronica said.

"Well, you get to be popular," Marissa said with a shrug. "Boys like you."

I thought about Brad, who wanted to be with me instead of Krystal. "Veronica's right," I told Marissa, "not always."

Marissa kept doodling, her head down. "That's easy for you guys to say, because you're pretty. I used to be pretty and now I'm not, so I know the difference." A startled look of pain flew across her face.

"Are you okay?" I asked her quickly.

"Something hurts," she said, alarm in her eyes. "Under my bandage, it doesn't feel right—"

"I'll get a nurse," I said quickly. I ran to the nurses' station and told Penny, the nurse on duty. She quickly followed me back to the kids' playroom.

"Hi, Marissa," Penny said. "What's up?"

"It feels like my nose is pushing on the bandage," Marissa said. "It hurts."

"That's probably just because the doctor reduced your pain medication today," Penny explained. "How about if I take you back to your room for a rest, and I'll ask the doctor to look in on you, okay?"

"Okay," Marissa agreed. "Will you guys come back and see me tomorrow?" she added hopefully.

"Count on it," Cindy promised.

She managed a smile with her strange looking mouth before Penny wheeled Marissa away.

"Marissa is the smartest nine year old I ever met in my life," Veronica marveled.

"She's incredible," Cindy agreed. "She's already got the world figured out."

"She's right about being pretty," I said thoughtfully.

Veronica stood up and paced across the room. "It just makes me so mad, though," she said. "All this stuff about looks and popularity. If Marissa wants to be a cheerleader, she should be able to be a cheerleader!"

Sometimes a great idea comes to me in a split second. Which is exactly what happened. I jumped out of my seat. "I'm brilliant!"

"And ego-free," Cindy teased me.

"You guys, I just got the most incredible idea!" I exclaimed. "We should have a Hope Hospital cheerleading squad! That way Marissa really *could* be a cheerleader! And just think about what great physical therapy it will be for the kids..."

"Most of them have trouble even walking," Cindy pointed out.

"So?" I said, warming up to my own idea. "Some of our cheerleaders will cheer from wheelchairs, it doesn't matter! The kids who are here for a long time can teach the kids who are here for a short time. And they can put on cheerleading shows for the staff and the other kids..."

"They'd have to have real cheerleading outfits," Veronica said thoughtfully.

"Maybe we could get some local business to donate them," Cindy added.

"We can do this!" I exclaimed. "I know we can do this! And I know the perfect person to coach our cheerleaders!"

"Not me," Cindy said. "I can teach them to do a cartwheel—well, the ones who are strong and mobile enough, anyway, but I'm really not the right person to—"

"Not you," I interrupted. "The newest patient on the Foxx Wing—Krystal Franklin!"

Chapter 9

"You guys, I don't think this is such a good idea," Cindy said hesitantly.

"It's a great idea," I insisted. "I'm sure of it."

It was three days later, after school, and Cindy, Veronica, and I were on our way to Krystal's room to ask her to lead the Hope Hospital Cheerleaders.

We had accomplished so much in three days, it was really amazing. When we told Dr. Dan our idea for official cheerleaders, he thought it was terrific. He called the National Sports Uniform Company in Delaware and somehow convinced the company to donate ten little cheerleading outfits! We were expecting them in the mail within the next few days.

The day before, we had held a meeting for all the kids interested in cheerleading—we decided guys should be able to be cheerleaders, too. Five girls and two boys showed up. When we told them about the Hope Hospital Cheerleaders, their faces lit up with excitement. We promised them a real cheerleader would be their coach. Now we just had to get that "real cheerleader" to agree.

None of us had seen Krystal yet—it was only the second day that she was allowed to have visitors other than her immediate family. Dawn had told Cindy at school that she'd been in to see her, but that's all she'd say. The nurses on Foxx Wing told me she was doing really well, physically, anyway. Rachel said she had a terrible attitude, but then Rachel's idea of a terrible attitude might just mean that Krystal wasn't hap-hap-happy all day long.

"Maybe we should just ask Dawn or one of the other cheerleaders to coach our kids," Veronica said as we walked to the Foxx Wing. A nurse pushed a girl on a stretcher by us, and we moved out of the way.

"But the whole point here is to do something that will help the kids and help Krystal, too," I reminded her.

Veronica shook her head. "I don't understand you, Tina Wu," she said softly. She had recently begun calling me by both of my names, just like Cindy and my grandmother.

"Me, either," Cindy agreed. "Krystal was horrible to you. She's a bigot. Why should you want to help her?"

I thought about that for a moment as we walked toward Krystal's room. "Well," I began slowly, "maybe if I do something that helps her, she won't be such a bigot anymore."

"But you don't have to prove yourself to her!" Veronica said.

"Yeah," Cindy agreed. "Do you expect her to say, 'Wow, I was so wrong to be mean to Tina Wu or to be mean to someone just because she's a different race from me'?"

"Maybe," I said truthfully.

"Well, in the words of your grandmother," Cindy replied, "'Tina Wu, you crazy!'"

I laughed. "Yeah, yeah, yeah, I already know that. Anyhow, let's figure out our game plan once we get into her room."

"How about if I say, 'Yo, Krystal, want to

be the cheerleading coach for the little kids here at the hospital?' and then she says 'no' and then we leave," Cindy suggested.

"Maybe she'll say yes," I said. "I mean, now she knows what it feels like to be a patient herself."

"You see the world through rose-colored glasses," Veronica told me.

"Well, red *is* my favorite color," I said with a grin. We were standing outside Krystal's door. "I guess we just wing it in there, okay?"

"Okay," Cindy agreed with a dubious shrug.

"Lead the way," Veronica said.

I knocked on the door to Krystal's room.

"Who is it?" she yelled.

I pointed at Cindy to answer her. I wasn't so sure Krystal would respond well to me.

"Cindy Winters," Cindy called in.

"Go away," Krystal yelled.

"Okay," Cindy said, eager to leave.

I shook my head no. "It's Tina," I called through the door. "And Veronica, too."

"All of you go away," Krystal called.

"Excuse me, girls, I have to go in and give Krystal her meds," a young nurse said. She opened the door and I peeked inside.

And I sucked in my breath.

Because Krystal Franklin looked like a monster.

Her face was covered in bandages. One eye was swollen shut. The other eye was blood red. Her head was shaved. Her mouth hung down on one side, pulled into an angry grimace by dark, livid-looking stitches.

"What the hell are you staring at?" Krystal yelled when she saw me staring at her. "I told you to leave!"

Hesitantly I walked into her room. Cindy and Veronica followed me. We just stood there while the nurse gave Krystal her medication, which she swallowed quickly with some water.

"We wanted to see how you're doing," Veronica said.

"Well, now you see," Krystal said bitterly. "Happy?"

"Of course not," I said, taking a step toward her bed. "We're really sorry this happened to you."

"Why should you care?" Krystal asked.

I couldn't think of a good answer.

"I suppose now that you've seen me you're going to tell everyone at school how I look," Krystal said, her red eye staring hard at Cindy.

"No—" Cindy began.

"Of course you will," Krystal snapped. "If it was you, I'd tell everyone. That's how people are. Dawn probably already told you I look like something from a freak show."

"No, she didn't," Cindy said firmly.

"Well, I do. I'm sure everyone is laughing big-time. I don't care. I don't care about anything." She turned her head away from us and stared out the window. "Look, just go away," she finally mumbled.

Cindy and Veronica looked at me. I could see they wanted to leave. But somehow I just couldn't. Not without even asking Krystal what we'd come to ask her.

I took a step toward her bed and cleared my throat. "We're starting a cheerleading squad here at the hospital," I said hesitantly. "You know, for the little kids in pediatrics."

"So?" Krystal asked, her head still turned toward the window.

I took a deep breath. "We arranged for them to get real cheerleading outfits and everything," I continued. "They're incredibly excited. And...uh...we promised them that a real cheerleader would be their coach." I looked at Cindy and Veronica for help, but they were both staring at me. "So…we wanted to know if you'd do it. Be their coach."

Krystal gave an ugly laugh and turned her head. "That's a good one."

"She wasn't joking," Veronica said.

"Well, she should have been," Krystal said.

"There's nothing wrong with your body," I pointed out. "I mean, you can still cheer."

Krystal didn't say a word.

"It would mean so much to the little kids," I continued. "They really loved it when you and the other cheerleaders demonstrated cheers for them that day."

"So ask one of the other cheerleaders, then," Krystal said.

"We could," Veronica agreed. "But the kids in here feel different from other kids. And we thought that since you're a patient here yourself, it would be really good for them to have you. You know, someone more like them—"

"Look, let's get this straight," Krystal said in a low voice. "I'm not like them. I'm nothing like them. I don't have a plucky attitude and I'm not going to overcome this."

"Sure you will—" I began.

"Shut up," Krystal interrupted me. "You don't know what you're talking about. I've seen what I look like. And all the plastic surgery in the world isn't going to make me pretty again."

"You don't know that," Cindy said.

"I do know that," Krystal insisted. "I'm ugly. Not just ugly. I'm...I'm a freak."

"But you don't have to take that attitude!" I exclaimed. "Look at Marissa—"

"You just don't get it!" Krystal cried. "I don't care about Marissa and her positive attitude. I don't care about any of them! Don't you understand? If I have to live like this, I'd rather be dead!"

I was so shocked I couldn't open my mouth.

"I want to die!" Krystal wailed. She grabbed the pillow and rocked her chest into it. "I just want to die!" She was sobbing, deep, racking sobs. I hesitated and then I moved toward her. She jerked her head back. "Don't you dare feel sorry for me!" she screamed, her livid red eye glaring at me. "Just get out of here! All of you! Get out! Get out!"

We hurried out of the room and closed the door behind us.

"Wow," Cindy breathed. "I didn't know what to say to her."

"We did what we could," Veronica said.

We walked down to the Foxes Den so we could talk. Two new girls, both in wheelchairs, were watching the big-screen TV. We sat on the other side of the room so we wouldn't disturb them.

"I don't think we should just...just give up," I said earnestly.

"Look, she has a right to her own feelings," Veronica pointed out. "Life isn't a fairy tale, and there isn't always a happy ending."

"But Tina Wu likes happy endings, don't you?" Cindy said with a smile. She tugged on a lock of my hair.

"Well, so?" I asked them. "You guys know it would be really good for Krystal. She'd have to stop thinking about herself long enough to think about the little kids!"

Cindy shrugged and threw her leg over the side of the chair. "Face it. Krystal was selfish and self-centered before her accident, and she's just the same now."

"Right," Veronica agreed. "The only difference is she isn't pretty anymore, so it's harder for her to get away with it."

I ran my finger along the edge of the table. "That's really not fair, is it," I said thoughtfully.

"Nope," Veronica said, twisting a lock of her hair around her finger. "Life isn't very fair at all. And I believe in staying out of a person's life if she doesn't want me in it."

"Me too," Cindy agreed. "So let's just figure out which of the cheerleaders we should ask to be the coach. How about Patti? She seems like the nicest cheerleader."

"Will you ask her?" I asked Cindy.

"Yeah, okay."

"Today?" I pressed. "Because the cheerleading outfits will be here in three days, and it would be so good for the kids if they could start right away and—"

"Tina Wu, give it a rest!" Cindy said with a laugh. "I'll ask her!"

Veronica looked at her watch. "Miss Jenkins is probably waiting for me in front of the hospital," she said. "Do you two want to come over for dinner? We could call Patti from my house." Miss Jenkins was the Langleys' housekeeper—house *manager* was really more like it—and often chauffered Veronica around, too.

"I can come," Cindy said quickly. "Dad is going to be home tonight, so I don't have to make dinner for Hei—"

Heidi. She was going to say Heidi. But

Heidi was a patient at the hospital. And she would be for a very, very long time.

"I know Heidi's in the hospital," Cindy finally said. "I just...forgot for a minute."

"It's okay," Veronica said quickly.

"I'm just so used to taking care of her..."

I got up and put my arms around Cindy. I didn't know what else to do. I knew that Cindy felt really guilty about Heidi's accident—she felt as if it was her fault, even though it wasn't.

"I'm okay, really," she said, shaking me off. "So, you want to eat at Veronica's? They have incredible food."

"How come you never want to talk about Heidi's accident?" I asked her.

"Because I just don't," she insisted.

"But don't you think—" I began.

"I said I don't want to talk about it," Cindy repeated.

"Okay."

Cindy got up. "I'll go find Dad and tell him I'm going to your house," Cindy told Veronica.

"I have to go home," I said with a sigh. "My grandmother cooked dinner. No one misses the meal when my grandmother cooks, unless they've been kidnapped, and only then with written permission."

"So I'll get Patti's number and call her from Veronica's house," Cindy said, "and we'll call you after that, okay?"

"Okay," I agreed.

"I'll meet you in front," Cindy told Veronica, and she bopped off to find her dad.

"I wish she'd talk about Heidi," I said to Veronica.

She smiled at me. "Tina Wu, you can't make everything okay for everybody, you know."

I smiled back. "I can try, can't I?"

"Okay, everybody, listen up!" I called out to the nine kids sitting in the pediatric lounge. "Today is a really big day for you guys!"

It was the next day, and we were about to have our very first cheerleading practice. The good news was that the little kids were really excited about it. The bad news was that none of the Hope Middle School cheerleaders had agreed to be the coach. No one had enough time, they said.

Which meant that Cindy got the job by default.

She wasn't too happy about it, either.

"Today we get to be cheerleaders, right?"

Marielle asked in a small, tired voice. It broke my heart to look at her. She was running fevers on a regular basis, and it seemed to me that she was losing ground daily. Still it seemed like nothing could break her spirit. When she heard we were having the first cheerleading practice, she absolutely insisted on being there.

"Right," I agreed. "So let's have a big welcome for your coach...Cindy!"

"She's my sister!" Heidi yelled proudly from her wheelchair.

I sort of pushed Cindy forward. She was wearing her gymnastics outfit with a sweatshirt over her leotard. She didn't exactly look like a cheerleader, but she looked cute.

Some of the kids clapped, but others just stared at us.

"I thought we were going to have a real cheerleader for our coach," Deena said.

"Cindy is a real cheerleader...sort of," Veronica said, trying to put a good spin on things.

"But you said you weren't a cheerleader," Kimber reminded us.

"Well, I'm not," Cindy admitted.

"But she could be," I said brightly. "Remember we told you guys how Cindy is a gymnast and everything, but she just decided not to try out for cheerleading."

"I'd rather have a real cheerleader," Kimber said petulantly.

"Yeah," Deena agreed.

"Don't say anything bad about my sister!" Heidi warned.

"Hey, I can teach you guys some great cheers," Cindy insisted. "You're going to be a terrific cheerleading squad!"

"It's stupid," Deena said.

Marielle looked sad. She wasn't feeling strong enough to go against Deena.

"No one wants to see a bunch of sick kids do cheers, anyway," a new girl named Debbie added.

"That's probably why none of the real cheerleaders would be our coach," Kimber said, kicking her good foot against the footlock on her wheelchair.

"Yeah," Deena agreed.

"You got boys in here?" Jerome asked, limping into the lounge.

"Sure!" I cried, even though at the moment there weren't any boys in the room. The two who had shown up for the other meeting had both chickened out.

Jerome looked around. "I don't see any boys."

"You're a boy," Deena said, giggling.

"I know that, woman!" Jerome growled.

"You can be a cheerleader," I told him. "There are plenty of guy cheerleaders."

"You must think I'm some kind of fool," Jerome snorted. "If my gang found out I was a cheerleader, they'd throw my sissy self out on my ear." He folded his arms. "I'll watch and decide who's the cutest."

"Jerome!" Cindy chastised him.

"The whole thing is stupid, anyway," Deena said. She turned to Marielle. "Let's go color, instead."

"But...maybe it'll be fun," Marielle said tentatively.

"I doubt it," Kimber put in. "We're just a bunch of losers. No one wants to see us do stupid cheers." She turned to Debbie. "Come on, Debbie. Let's go to my room."

Various kids started to straggle away, some on foot, others wheeling in their chairs. Heidi looked crestfallen. It looked like my big idea was going to be a big bust.

Until Marissa stood up.

"I want to be a cheerleader," she said in her muffled voice.

"Well, you're the only one, then," Kimber called from the doorway.

"I don't care," Marissa said. "Cindy and I

will be the Hope Hospital Cheerleaders if no one else wants to. What color are our outfits, Cindy?"

"Red and white," Cindy said, loud enough so even the kids who had reached the hallway could hear her. "And the sweaters are embroidered with the word 'Hope' on the front."

Debbie took a couple of steps back into the room. "Does the sweater say the word 'Hospital' after the word 'Hope'?" she asked.

"No," I replied.

"We were thinking that our cheerleaders could cheer during the Tiger baseball game on Saturday afternoon," Veronica said. "We could put the game on the big TV in the Foxes Den..."

"And all the teens from up there would be there?" Kimber asked.

"Absolutely," I assured her. "And some other guys who aren't even patients at the hospital."

"How could we learn to be cheerleaders that fast?" Debbie asked.

"Because Cindy is a really, really great coach," Marissa said. "Right, Cindy?"

"Right," Cindy agreed, smiling at Marissa.

Jerome looked at Marielle. "You'd better

do it," he advised her. "The squad needs a babe like you, and that's the truth."

Marielle giggled, her painfully thin face lighting up for a moment. "I want to do it," she said.

"Me too," Debbie agreed.

"Yeah, me too," Kimber said.

"Let's start now," Deena added.

"Hurrah!" Heidi yelled.

"You got it," Cindy agreed. "All Hope Cheerleaders, front and center!"

And the first official practice of the Hope Hospital Cheerleaders began.

That evening I was sitting in my room, supposedly doing my history homework, but really I was doodling in the corner of my notebook and thinking about how well the first cheerleading practice had gone.

Cindy had taught the girls two different cheers. Most of it was done with the upper body so that everyone could do it. The biggest surprise came when we found out that Marissa could do a cartwheel, and the splits! She had surprised everybody, and we all clapped and carried on about how wonderful she was. She said she'd been practicing by herself in her room!

There was a knock on my bedroom door.

"Come in," I called.

"Tina Wu, phone call for you," my grandmother said with a frown.

"I didn't hear it," I replied, looking at my phone extension.

Grandmother walked over to the phone and found out it was unplugged. "This good reason," she said.

"Oh, I guess I forgot," I told her. "Thanks." I plugged my phone back in and waited for her to leave my room so that I could pick up the receiver.

"It boy," she told me, and she didn't sound any too thrilled about it.

Brad! It had to be Brad!

"Thanks, Grandmother," I said.

She didn't move.

"Who this boy?" she demanded.

"How do I know, I didn't answer the phone yet," I pointed out.

She harrumphed under her breath and left the room. I snatched up the phone. "Hello?"

"Hi, Tina, it's Brad."

"Hi," I said happily.

"So, how you doin'?" he asked.

"I'm good. We had the first cheerleading practice at the hospital today. The kids were so cute." I went on and told him all about how Cindy was the coach, and how well everyone had done. "We're planning to have the kids cheer Saturday afternoon in the Foxes Den," I continued. "We figured we'd put the Tigers game on the big TV."

"Great idea," Brad agreed.

"So do you want to come?" I blurted out. Well, you know me, I'm not shy. No guts, no glory, I always say!

"Sure," Brad said. "If I can."

"You might be busy?" I asked, feeling disappointed.

"My parents want to take me to this famous hospital in St. Louis where they specialize in heart surgery for kids," he said.

"You should go," I told him.

"Why, so more doctors can tell me I need to have surgery?"

"If you need it, you need it," I said firmly.

"I'm doing okay without it," Brad said defensively.

"But you told me yourself you can't run, you can't dance, you can't do sports..."

"So?" Brad said. "Sometimes you can't do stuff because of your lupus. That's just the way it is."

"There's no surgery that can make lupus better," I said. "But I can tell you this. If there was, I'd have it."

I could hear Brad breathing into the phone.

"Brad?"

"Hmmmmm?"

"It's okay to be scared, you know."

"Yeah," he finally murmured.

"So, if you're not in St. Louis, I guess I'll see you Saturday, right?"

"Right," he agreed. "And just remember the Saturday after that is my school dance."

"I won't forget," I promised.

We hung up the phone, and I threw myself down on the bed so I could think about what just happened. Brad's school dance. How was I ever going to get my parents and my grandparents—mostly my grandmother—to let me go?

There was a knock on the door.

I sighed. I knew who it was. "Come in," I said.

"Who was that boy?" my grandmother asked.

"A friend," I explained. "I met him at the hospital. His name is Brad Kennedy."

"Not Chinese?" grandmother asked.

"No," I admitted.

"He nice boy?"

"So nice," I told her earnestly. "He's smart

and polite and he comes from a very good family."

Actually I had no idea what kind of family Brad came from, but I knew this would be a key factor with my grandmother.

She did that harrumphing thing under her breath again. I crossed my fingers and hoped for the best. "Actually, Grandmother, he...he invited me to a dance at his school. A week from Saturday." I held my breath.

"You too young to date," she said firmly.

"Well, it's not a date, really," I said quickly. "I mean, a whole bunch of kids will be going. We'll be going with a...a group," I invented. "So it's not a date."

Grandmother narrowed her eyes and looked pensive. "You invite boy to dinner," she decided. "Then we see."

Oh, no! I couldn't invite Brad to dinner! I couldn't imagine him having to go through the drill he'd get from my grandmother or my parents. And my grandfather would just sit there eating, pretending Brad didn't even exist. And then my brother and sisters...they would find endless ways to mortify me. No, I just couldn't do it! There had to be another way!

"You don't invite him to meet family, you don't go to dance," Grandmother declared.

There was no use arguing with her. I knew my parents would totally go along with whatever she decreed.

"Okay, Grandmother," I agreed. "I'll invite Brad to dinner."

"Saturday," she said. Then she looked around my room. "Tina Wu, clean up mess!" she added. Then she turned on her heel and marched out.

By twelve-thirty Saturday afternoon there was a crowd of more than forty people in the Foxes Den—family, friends, nurses, therapists, doctors, and of course me, Veronica, and Cindy. Cindy and her cheerleaders were in the kitchen area behind a sheet that had been made into a curtain separating them from the rest of us.

Rachel, Virginia, and some of the other nurses had made a bunch of food, and they had set it up on a long table. Trevor was there, making himself a sandwich from the deli stuff.

Brad wasn't there, and he hadn't called me. I didn't know what that meant. Was he mad about what I'd said to him on the phone the other day? Had he gone to St. Louis without even telling me? What if he didn't like me anymore? But I refused to let myself think like that. Brad and I were friends. A friend is someone you can tell the truth to.

"Are you nervous?" Veronica asked me, sipping at a paper cup of fruit punch.

"No, they're going to be great," I assured her.

"I was just back there," she told me. "The kids are scared to death."

"But everyone is going to love them!" I exclaimed. "Everyone already *does* love them!"

"I know that," Veronica said thoughtfully. "But I think they want people to think they're great cheerleaders, and not just because they feel sorry for them."

"No pity party, you mean," I translated.

"Right," Veronica said.

I looked around. "I notice Krystal isn't here."

"You didn't really think she'd come, did you?" Veronica said softly.

"No, I guess not," I admitted, "but maybe

it's because no one invited her." I looked at my watch. "We still have fifteen minutes before they start..."

"Come on, Tina Wu," Veronica said, "you need to give it a rest."

"Oh, what's the biggie," I said. "I'll just go invite her, and if she says no, she says no."

"She will," Veronica predicted.

I hurried out of the Foxes Den and went straight to Krystal's room. Her door was open, but I knocked anyway.

"What?" she said, staring at me. I noticed one eye looked almost normal now, and her face wasn't as swollen and purple-looking. But she still looked terrible.

"I thought I'd invite you down to the lounge," I told her. "The Hope Hospital Cheerleaders are cheering for the first time."

"I know all about it," Krystal said. "Everyone's been talking about it all week."

"Want to come?"

"No, I don't want to come," Krystal said. "Isn't that obvious?"

"Well, okay. I just wanted you to know that we want you there," I told her.

"You don't want me there any more than I want to be there," Krystal snapped. "So let's not lie to each other."

"That's not true—"

"Yes, it is. Unless you want me there so you can feel superior."

"I don't feel superior," I said quietly.

"Look, don't lie about it," Krystal snapped. "I know what it's like when you're good-looking and someone is a dog. I always felt superior to girls like that."

"Everyone isn't like you," I pointed out.

"Well, the laugh's on me, huh," Krystal said bitterly. "Now I'm not just a dog, I'm a monster."

"No, you're not," came a small, muffled voice from the doorway.

I turned around. It was Marissa, in her red and white cheerleading outfit. There was a red ribbon in her hair, and a red heart painted on the bandage across her nose.

"I came to see you," Marissa said. She walked over to Krystal's bed and sat down. "The cheerleaders are cheering today for the first time. I'm kind of nervous."

"It'll be okay," Krystal said gruffly. "I'm always nervous at the first game of the season."

"Really?" Marissa asked wide-eyed.

"Yeah," Krystal replied. "Once you get going you'll forget all about it."

"I remember what you taught me that day," Marissa said. "You know, about spirit and everything."

Krystal nodded.

"I was hoping maybe you'd come see us cheer," Marissa said, "since you're a real cheerleader and everything."

"I can't," Krystal said. She turned her face away from us.

Marissa put her hand on the covers over Krystal's knee. "It's because you don't want people to stare at your face," she said. "I understand. But that day you came and taught us cheers, I found out I really *could* be a cheerleader, remember? You told me that if I was tough and I had the spirit, I could do it, and I did!"

"It's not the same for me," Krystal said, keeping her head averted toward the window. I could hear the tears in her voice, and her shoulders were shaking. "The only reason anyone ever liked me was because I was pretty. If I'm not pretty, I'm nothing!"

Marissa bit at her lower lip and thought for a moment. "If you're tough and you've got the spirit, you're not nothing," she finally said.

Krystal didn't respond, though I could see her swipe the back of her hand along her cheek to wipe away her tears.

"Come on, honey," I told Marissa. "You tried."

We hurried back to the Foxes Den, where Veronica was frantically waving to us. "Hurry up!" she hissed. "Cindy has been looking all over for Marissa! They're ready to start!"

"I'm ready," Marissa assured Veronica. She hurried behind the sheet with the rest of the cheerleaders.

"Okay, now I'm nervous," I confessed, squeezing Veronica's hand.

"I'll say, your hands are freezing," Veronica said. "Well, it's show time!" She turned the sound down on the big-screen TV and motioned for Jerome to come forward.

"Ladies and gentlemen, dudes and dudettes, foxes of all ages," Jerome announced. "It is my pleasure to introduce, for the first time, the debut performance of the one, the only, the coolest, the baddest Ladies of Hope, the Hope-ettes!"

Veronica and I quickly opened the curtain, and the Hope-ettes, each in her red and white cheerleading uniform, ran, hobbled, or wheeled their way into the room to thunderous applause and whistles.

They formed a raggedy line with Marissa front and center. She looked over at Cindy, who gave her an encouraging nod, then Marissa looked out at the crowd. She put her hands on her hips. "Ready? Begin!"

WE'RE THE HOPE-ETTES
AND WE'RE PROUD TO SAY
WE'RE CHEERING THE TIGERS
ON TODAY.
WE'RE REALLY TOUGH
AND WE'VE GOT THE SPIRIT.
WE'RE ALL WINNERS,
YOU'D BETTER BELIEVE IT!

As the girls cheered, they bopped together in perfect unison. The kids who were mobile did some spins and leaps. The kids in wheelchairs managed to dance with their upper bodies, jiving to the funky beat of the cheer.

The cheer ended with all the cheerleaders spelling *Hope-ettes*. Then Marissa did her famous cartwheel and finished in the splits, with all the other cheerleaders pointing to her.

The place went wild with applause, whistles, and cheers of appreciation. And I was cheering loudest of all.

"Hi," a voice said next to me.

Brad! I was so happy to see him that before I could stop myself, I threw my arms around him in a big hug.

"I'm so glad to see you!" I cried. "Did you see that? Weren't they wonderful?"

Brad grinned at me. "You're the one who's wonderful," he said in a low voice. "But yeah, they're pretty wonderful, too. Hey, guess who's in the hallway."

"Tinker Bell?" I guessed.

Brad laughed. "No, she's sitting over there on the couch with Dr. Dan, looking very cozy. Krystal's in the hallway."

"She is?" I turned around. And there she was, standing just outside the room, half hiding behind the door.

"I'll be right back," I told Brad. I walked over to Krystal. "Hi."

"Hi," she said.

"I'm glad you came," I told her.

She shrugged.

"You can come in, you know," I said.

"No," she said in a low voice.

The cheerleaders were getting ready for their next cheer. Krystal watched Marissa as she got into her place. "She's an incredible kid, isn't she."

"She is," I agreed. "She's tough, and she's got the spirit."

"Those are just words," Krystal said wearily.

"No, they aren't," I insisted. "Not if you really mean them."

The kids began their second cheer. "I'm not like her," Krystal said. "I'm not an incredible person that everyone is going to admire."

"Maybe you just never gave yourself the chance to be," I said.

Krystal folded her arms and jutted her chin at me. "I totally don't get you at all," she admitted.

"Yeah, I don't always get me, either," I agreed.

"You should hate me," Krystal said.

I shrugged. "What would be the point?"

She stared at me a moment. "One of the nurses told me that you have some disease called lupus."

I nodded.

"She said you've spent a lot of time as a patient here," Krystal continued.

I nodded again.

"So, does this lupus thing hurt?" Krystal asked, her voice guarded.

"Sometimes," I replied.

She shifted her weight. "Can you die from it?"

It felt as if a fist was clenched around my

heart. Because this is a question no one had ever asked me before. Not out loud. My parents never talked about it. But I knew the truth, even though it was one I tried not to ever think about.

"Yeah," I said. "You can die from it." I stuck my hair behind one ear. "But I don't plan on dying from it, you know," I added.

"You look normal," Krystal said, and there was envy in her voice.

"I don't even know what 'normal' means," I said. "Everyone has something wrong with them. Some people's stuff just shows, and some people's doesn't."

"I guess you never know..." Krystal said, staring at Marissa.

"Yeah," I said, and I looked over at Marissa, too. "I know just what it feels like when you don't want anyone to feel sorry for you."

She didn't respond, she just watched Marissa, out there cheering her heart out. "She needs some work on that jump-back move," Krystal said. "Her back isn't straight enough. And her shoulders need to roll on the offbeat, it looks much hipper that way."

"You could teach her sometime," I said casually.

"Maybe I will," Krystal said half to

herself. "Maybe I just will."

I walked back over to Brad, and I slipped my hand into his. He turned to me and smiled, then he squeezed my hand and held on to it tight.

Right at that moment, with the Hope Hospital Hope-ettes cheering, and Brad's hand in mine, I realized that what Marissa had said was true. If you had spirit and you were tough, then you really were something. Something pretty terrific. It was *definitely* the kind of person I wanted to be.

And while nothing was perfect—I still didn't know what Brad was going to do about his surgery, and I couldn't get Cindy to talk about how guilty she felt about Heidi's accident, and Veronica still seemed to practically hate her mother for divorcing her father, and I would always have my scary, who-knew-what-would-happen lupus—everything seemed at least...well...at least *possible.*

"Hey, Tina Wu," Brad said.

"What?"

"About dinner at your family's tonight," Brad said.

"Uh-huh?"

"I'm there."

"Oh. Good," I told him. Half of me was glad, and the other half of me was not ready to face the horror of Brad facing my family.

Because the only person tougher and more spirited than me was my grandmother.

"I can handle it," I mumbled out loud. "After all, I'm her granddaughter!"

"What?" Brad asked.

"Oh, nothing," I said innocently.

When the Hope-ettes finished their last cheer and took a bow, there was Marissa, front and center, her head held high.

I changed my mind. Grandmother wasn't the toughest and most spirited of all.

That title belonged to a little nine-year-old girl named Marissa Ruiz.

Dear Cherie,

You are my favorite author. I love your books because they are so realistic. The character of Jerome made me laugh and Brianna made me cry. I have a suggestion. Maybe Veronica and Cindy could become sisters when their parents marry each other! What do you think? Also, how did you get so much info on hospitals?

Your real #1 fan,

Kate Kelly
Austin, Texas

Dear Kate,

Thanks for picking me as your favorite author! That makes my day! Look for much *more romance ahead for Veronica's mom and Cindy's dad. Do you readers think they make a good couple? Would it be good or bad for Veronica and Cindy to become sisters? As to your second question, I did a lot of research on hospitals in preparation for this series. I am constantly thumbing through a book called* Teens and Health. *Also, my brother-in-law is a doctor in New York, and I call him all the time with questions. Thanks for reading!*

Best

Cherie

Dear Cherie,

I really loved HOPE HOSPITAL, GET WELL SOON, LITTLE SISTER. I laughed and I cried. It was the best book I ever read. Here is a question: how do you get the ideas for your books?

Robby S. Sasser
Nashville, Tennessee

Dear Robby,

Thanks for all the compliments! I'm always psyched to get mail from guys as well as girls. I get my ideas from my own life, from friends, from talk shows, and from readers. Actually, I've gotten some of my very best ideas from fan letters! I have heard from a number of kids who were sick or injured and had to be in the hospital for extended periods of time. They told me how much my books meant to them, and also how important it was for them to have friends who stuck by them while they were sick. Hey, true friendship needs to come through in the tough times, right?

Best

Cherie

Dear Readers,

Wow, you guys are so great! I have already gotten so many wonderful letters about HOPE HOSPITAL that it was difficult to pick the two I printed in this book. Keep those letters, cards, and photos coming, okay? I just love to hear from you!

Many of you have written to ask if Hope, Michigan, and Hope Hospital really exist. The answer is no, they don't—except in my imagination! I have never lived in a really small town like Hope—but I'd love to hear from those of you out there who do! You can help me get the details right!

It really is possible for you guys to do volunteer work at a hospital, you know. You can call your local hospital and ask for more information. Little kids who are stuck in the hospital would love it if you would visit them. Hey, just think about how much it would mean to you if you were the patient!

We all know that everyone has struggles and problems, right? For some people, it's physical, like a handicap or an illness. For other people, it's mental or emotional. Some people's problems show on the outside and other people's problems are more hidden in the inside. But whatever your problems are, you are not alone, even though it might feel that way sometimes. Please always remember that I care. You can write to me, and I'll listen. And I promise to write you back personally.

Question for the day...What is the worst advice an adult ever gave you?

So, how do we write to you, Cherie? Send mail to: Cherie Bennett, PO Box 150326, Nashville, Tennessee 37215. I can't wait to hear from you!

Best,

Cherie

Coming in May 1996 to a bookstore near you, another wonderful HOPE HOSPITAL book:

The Initiation

Is Veronica trying too hard to fit in?

The Gold Girls are the snobbiest group at school, and Veronica isn't even sure she really likes them. But there's something so appealing about belonging to a special club, especially now when Veronica's begun to feel she doesn't really belong *anywhere.* Her mother is always so wrapped up in her busy job at the hospital. Her father spends all his time with his new family; his second wife even has a daughter Veronica's age. Veronica feels so unwanted—except by the Gold Girls. But Veronica has to prove she's Gold Girl material by accepting a dangerous dare. Can Veronica get away with it—or will she end up regretting it the rest of her life?

Available wherever you buy books.

Troll 0-8167-3914-5 / $3.95 U.S. / $5.50 CAN.

Cherie Bennett is one of the best-selling authors for young adults and middle-grade readers in the world, with more than three million books in print, in many languages. She is also one of America's finest young playwrights, whose award-winning plays about teens, JOHN LENNON & ME and ANNE FRANK & ME, are being produced around the world. She lives in Nashville, Tennessee, with her husband, Jeff Gottesfeld, a film and theater producer and writer, and their two fat cats, Julius and Trinity.

Photo by David Frohman